The Curse
of the Shaman

For
AJ

Michael

The Curse
of the Shaman

A Marble Island Story

MICHAEL KUSUGAK

with illustrations by Vladyana Krykorka

HarperTrophyCanada™
An imprint of HarperCollinsPublishersLtd

Published by Harper*Trophy*Canada™, an imprint of HarperCollins Publishers Ltd

Harper*Trophy*Canada™ is a trademark of HarperCollins Publishers.

First edition

HarperCollins books may be purchased for educational, business, or sales
promotional use through our Special Markets Department.

HarperCollins Publishers Ltd
2 Bloor Street East, 20th Floor
Toronto, Ontario, Canada
M4W 1A8

www.harpercollins.ca

Library and Archives Canada Cataloguing in Publication

Kusugak, Michael
    The curse of the shaman / Michael Kusugak. — 1st ed.

ISBN-13: 978-0-00-639512-6
ISBN-10: 0-00-639512-0

    I. Title.

PS8571.U83C87 2006   jC813'.54   C2005-905576-6

HC 9 8 7 6 5

Printed and bound in the United States
Design by Sharon Kish
Set in New Aster

I dedicate this book to my granddaughter, Taylor Arnakuluk Anguiliq Kusugak, the second breath of my life. I don't know how I ever got along without her. Now, my life is complete.

Preface

If you stand on a high hill in Rankin Inlet, a small community halfway up the western shore of Hudson Bay in Canada, and look east, way east, past Thomson Island—what we Inuit call Igluligjuaq, The-big-island-with-the-igloo—past Falstaff Island, called Ukkusiksat, or Soapstone—you will see a mirage, yes, a real mirage, a shimmering white island that floats just above the horizon. What you see is Marble Island. It lies forty-five kilometres straight out to sea.

Marble Island is seventeen kilometres long, lying east-west, and four kilometres wide. It is comprised almost entirely of white stone, quartzite, from which it gets its name.

In Inuktitut, the language of the inhabitants of the new Canadian territory of Nunavut where the island lies, it is called Uqsuriak—meaning Oil Slick—because from a distance, that is what it looks like: oil floating on water.

Marble Island is steeped in exploration and whaling history. In the early 1700s an explorer, James Knight, looking for the Northwest Passage and the riches that he imagined lay beyond, is believed to have perished on the island, along with his two ships and crew of forty men. Three hundred years later, you can still see the outline of his brick house at the east end of the island, covered in sod and overgrown with tundra grasses. His two ships remain in their silty, murky, watery grave at Eastend Harbour, a testament to the unrelenting, unforgiving harshness of the elements and Knight's unfounded fear of the Inuit.

From the mid-1700s to the early 1900s, Marble Island was a favourite anchoring place for whaling ships hunting the bowhead and right whales. Sunken ships, anchor chain, barrel hoops, graves, and other signs of human occupation can still be seen on and around the island.

Marble Island is also shrouded in folklore. A strange custom awaits you: you have to crawl up the beach on your hands and knees when you set foot on it for the first time. They say if you don't, you will be dead within a year. The reason for this custom is not known. It may be to pay homage to the old woman who was cast off on the ice floe that, legend says, became Marble Island. Or it may be to show respect to the explorers and whalers who died there, crawling on their hands and knees, victims of the dreaded scurvy. Or it may be for some other reason lost to history. But whatever the reason for the custom, you are wise not to tempt fate: better to suffer the small inconvenience of crawling up the beach and being sure of surviving another year.

But we are getting ahead of ourselves. That is a story for another day. Wolverine lived long before the explorers and whalers came. This is a story of his people.

Wolverine Is Born

Qabluittuq, The-man-with-no-eyebrows, was happy. He had a son, his very first child. Tonight, his wife, Can't-see, was nursing the new baby. The little boy had a wrinkled face and black, slick hair, sticking out in all directions. The-man-with-no-eyebrows sat on the bed beside his wife, holding the baby's hands.

"Atausiq, marruuk, pingasut . . . qulit!" he counted the tiny fingers. "One, two, three . . . ten!" he exclaimed.

He took the baby's feet: "Atausiq, marruuk, pingasut . . . qulit!" he counted the tiny toes. "One, two, three . . . ten!" he shouted again. "A perfect boy!" The-man-with-no-eyebrows was a happy man, indeed.

Can't-see asked, "What shall we call him?"

"We will call him Qavvik—Wolverine," The-man-with-no-eyebrows said. "We will name him after my father."

"Sakiga," Can't-see said, looking lovingly at the baby. "My father-in-law."

The-man-with-no-eyebrows took his naked baby in his huge hands and held him up above his head, close to the ceiling of the igloo. Wolverine was a beautiful baby with very dark skin, slightly blue from the cold. He had what looked like bruises on his back, just above his tiny bum; all Inuit are born with bruises like that. His eyes were closed. His short arms and legs flailed like he was trying to fly. The-man-with-no-eyebrows danced around and around, holding his baby up in the air.

"My father," he said to the little boy, "I am so happy you are here again."

"You'd better let me have him," Can't-see said. "He will get cold."

It was only then that The-man-with-no-eyebrows realized it was cold in his igloo, cold enough to see his breath. Igloos are never very warm.

"Aittaa!" he shouted. "How foolish of me. Of course."

He handed the baby back to his wife. Can't-see tucked Wolverine under her amaut—her caribou-skin baby-carrying coat. She looked up at her husband. He seemed so serious, concerned, and a little embarrassed. A smile raised the ends of her mouth; there was no harm done. She giggled. Then The-man-with-no-eyebrows and his wife laughed until their stomachs hurt and tears flowed from their eyes. Wolverine was their first baby. They were just learning to have a family.

"Turn up the qulliq," The-man-with-no-eyebrows said. "We have plenty of seal fat, and soon spring will come."

The qulliq was their only source of heat throughout the winter. It was a heavy hunk of soapstone carved in a half-moon shape with a depression on the top to hold the seal oil. Can't-see took her carved soapstone wick-adjusting prod and gently raised the wick, pulling it up the lip of the qulliq. The flames licked higher and a warm glow filled the igloo. She felt a little guilty, turning up the flame so much, but her husband had said there was plenty of seal oil. It was her habit to conserve every bit of seal fat that she could. During a very cold winter, their survival could depend on it.

The-man-with-no-eyebrows went outside to look at the end of the day. Spring was coming. The sun stayed longer in the sky now, climbing higher above the horizon each day. He stood there through the dusk, thinking happy thoughts of life yet to come. A light breeze blew from the west, soft and warmish on his tanned face. Already, there must be bare ground to the west that heated up with the sun through the day, making the west wind smell earthy and feel warm to the skin.

He stood there until the light of dusk faded and the great expanse of the ice on Hudson Bay disappeared with the coming darkness. The air became crisp and clear. The first stars appeared in the big ceiling of sky above him. *Tomorrow will be another good day,* he thought. One of his dogs, lying on the snow, stretched her legs way out, looked up at him, and yawned a fitful yawn. The-man-with-no-eyebrows shivered in his caribou-skin shirt. The fur was thinning from constant use, just in time for spring and summer. His clothes would be cool in the heat of the coming seasons.

Tomorrow, he decided, they would travel south to the point of land called Siuraarjuk—Bit-of-sand. Just to the south of Bit-of-sand was a white island. The island is called Uqsuriak, or Oil Slick, because from a distance, that is what it looks like: shiny oil floating on water. One day, many, many years from now, people from across the big ocean to the east would come, and they would call it by a new name; they would call it Marble Island. They would call it Marble Island because they thought the island looked as white as the marble of an Italian statue.

The-man-with-no-eyebrows' father had taken him there when he was a young man. They had hunted beluga whales and narwhals around the island. They had explored the caves.

The-man-with-no-eyebrows had seen the giant whales in the deep waters, just east of the island. He had seen the spray and the warm mist that followed as they blew air out through the tops of their massive heads. He had watched them breach, flying way up into the air and crashing down, splashing water all around. Arviit, they are called—bowhead whales. They are huge, but sometimes they clung to the shores of Marble Island, hiding from the ravenous aarlut—the orcas, killer whales. He would take his father there again; it was his turn.

The-man-with-no-eyebrows had eyebrows, of course, just as Can't-see could actually see; that was just his name. It was a good name. It had been passed down from generation to generation until it came to him. The first The-man-with-no-eyebrows probably had no eyebrows at all, or maybe his eyebrows were so faint that people had started to call him "The-man-with-no-eyebrows." It had probably started as a nickname, finally becoming his name when people forgot what his real name was.

Sometimes men had the name; sometimes women had it. Whether it was a man or a woman did not matter. What mattered was that the spirit of the person was carried on. Whomever the name came to had the responsibility of giving rebirth to the person behind the name. When he or she was gone, it was passed down to someone else as long as the name had been given dignity during the person's lifetime. The-man-with-no-eyebrows lived as best he could so that one day, when he was gone, a kindly mother and father would find it in their hearts to name their child after him, a worthy man. And the name, The-man-with-no-eyebrows, would survive another generation.

And now, Wolverine, his father, was reborn. It was a time of great happiness. The-man-with-no-eyebrows' heart filled with love and visions of his father, the elder Wolverine. He would teach Wolverine to hunt the smaller beluga whales and narwhals. He would teach his son to survive until he became a man.

The-man-with-no-eyebrows smiled. It was time to move, he thought. It was time to go and look for a wife for his son. There would be people at Bit-of-sand, people with baby girls for his son to marry. Tomorrow, they would head that way.

He looked once more at the darkening sky. He wiped his eyes with his hands. Tears had formed with the stinging cold of the evening air. As he went inside to his wife and his baby, his chest swelled with pride.

A Family at Last

Can't-see had come from the big island to the east called Salliq—Farther-out-to-sea. Her family were great seafarers, making their living fishing and hunting in the middle of the big bay, known simply as Salt. They ventured out to other islands in their kayaks and umiaqs—skin boats—sometimes reaching the other side of the bay in search of seals, walruses, whales, and polar bears. And there were plenty of walruses and polar bears on Farther-out-to-sea and the islands beyond. Can't-see's parents and her brothers and sisters were still there.

But her husband was a mainlander, which was why they lived here, on the mainland. She was happy here. Somehow, her family would find out about her son. It would not take long. They would meet other people in their nomadic travels, all over the land and the sea ice. Those people would tell others that she and The-man-with-no-eyebrows had a son. People would pass the word along, and soon, everyone would know there was a new boy called Wolverine. Can't-see looked at the new baby nestled in her arms with pride, love, and a new sense of responsibility.

She had given birth to him during the day when her husband was out hunting seals at the floe edge. To her, that seemed to be the way things were done: when it was time for a woman to give birth, the men went out hunting and the women stayed to assist with the birth.

But Can't-see had given birth on her own. There were no other women about to help her. It had been difficult, but she had been prepared. Alone in her igloo, she had surrounded herself with caribou skins, rolled up to support her arms and her back. And then she had brought Wolverine, a moving, breathing baby boy out into the world. There was no magic in the world that could be better than that.

She had lain there, just looking at her baby. She had carried this beautiful boy inside her body for months. He had grown until she could feel him move, hard little feet kicking her stomach out from the inside. And now, here he was, in person. She had marvelled at her baby boy, until she remembered she was not yet finished. Painfully, she had gotten up; it was hard work, having a baby. She had cleaned up the igloo. Then, walking on wobbly legs, she had taken the old caribou-skin bedding down to the sea where it would go out with the ice in spring. When she was finished, she was relieved. This was her job and she had done it. She could not help smiling about that. Holding Wolverine's tiny hand in hers and watching him suck on her breast, she had fallen asleep briefly, overcome by a tiredness like she had never felt before. The return of her husband had woken her from her sleep.

Here they were, all together. Her eyes twinkled in the glow of the qulliq. This was what she had wanted ever since she was a little girl, playing house outside her mother's tent: a family. She had a good husband and a baby boy; she had a family.

"Tomorrow, we will go south and find a nuliaksaq, a wife-to-be, for him," The-man-with-no-eyebrows said. "We will go to Bit-of-sand."

"Yes," Can't-see said. "He must have a wife-to-be."

That night, Can't-see and The-man-with-no-eyebrows woke many times, just to look at their son and smile in the faint glow of the qulliq. With the sun's first rays licking the dome of their igloo, they finally fell into a short but fitful sleep.

Paaliaq Has a Bad Day

Sitting in his igloo with his wife, Auk, and his elderly mother at Bit-of-sand, Paaliaq was not a happy man. His daughter was crying and he did not know why. He should have known, of course; he was an angakkuq—a shaman—after all. But he was a man, and men never know much about babies.

Paaliaq did not like to hear his baby crying. He bounced her on his lap and listened to her wail. He wanted her, so much, to be a happy girl. But her crying filled his igloo.

They called her Anirniq—Breath. She was such a beautiful baby. Just to look at her made Paaliaq sigh. Her hair was long and black. She had big brown eyes that flickered when she smiled. She had long, jet-black eyelashes that seemed to leave shadows on her eyelids.

Already, she opened her eyes and smiled if you said "Apuu!" And she smiled so beautifully. But she wasn't smiling now. She was crying as loud as she could.

"She just needs to exercise her voice," Paaliaq's elderly mother said.

"Oh," Paaliaq said. "But, Mother, why does she have to do it by crying?"

Paaliaq was a good man. He was a good shaman. He tried to help people with his special gift. But now and then, some people said he was a teeny, tiny bit short-tempered. And that made him mad. He wasn't short-tempered, he'd say; he just had a lot of things on his mind.

And Paaliaq did have a lot of things on his mind. He was a storyteller, entertaining people all over this huge land. He guided people to places where the hunting would be good. He showed people what the future would be like. And he helped people cure themselves of their sicknesses. Being a shaman was a very demanding job.

Paaliaq wore his long, black hair in braids. Tied to the tips of his braids were two small tails, carved out of walrus-tusk ivory. He had worn them as far back as he could remember. His mother said that his father had made them for him long ago. They were his symbols, signifying that he was a shaman. He was the youngest and smallest of his six brothers and sisters. He was also his mother's favourite, which was why she had come to live with him after Paaliaq's father had died. He was always a bit fat, but he was very strong and agile. There was a story people told about him:

Once, while he was out hunting seals on the sea ice, Paaliaq had come upon a huge polar bear. He had stopped his dogs. He had undone the carved ivory clasp, the sanniruaq, which held the dogs' lines to his sled, and let them loose. The dogs had immediately surrounded the bear, their sharp teeth bared, barking incessantly, nipping at the bear's flanks, jumping out of the way when it turned and swiped at them with its huge paws. This was the way you hunted polar bears. And Paaliaq's dogs knew how to hunt polar bears.

Protected by his dogs, Paaliaq had approached the bear. It was a male, very big and very fast. It was not happy with the dogs snarling all around him. It charged at them, swiping at them with its huge paws, turning on its flanks when a dog snapped at it from behind. Paaliaq had thrown his spear at it but the tip was dull and a bear's skin is thick and tough. The spear had just bounced off the bear's breast and landed on the snow nearby.

Now, trying to protect its rear end from the dogs, which were attacking from all sides, the bear turned and sat down on the snow. As luck would have it, it sat right down on Paaliaq's spear. *What to do?* Paaliaq asked himself, running here and there, skirting the dogs with the bear fending them off in the middle, taking care not to get tangled up in the dogs' lines, which were splayed all around.

Paaliaq took his mitts off and threw them down on the ground; he wanted to have a good grip. He rubbed his hands together. He stretched his fingers out as far as he could and then balled them into fists. He flexed his muscles and stamped his feet on the ground, making sure his body was in perfect working order. He shook his head to clear it. He needed to concentrate on the task at hand; he needed to be fast and strong.

He crouched down and sneaked around the bear, trying not to attract its attention. The bear was preoccupied with the dogs. When he was directly behind it, he ran quickly through the barking dogs, jumping over one of them, taking care not to get his feet entangled in the lines. He grabbed the bear's short tail and lifted it, holding on with all his might, so that the bear could not turn on him. As he lifted the bear's rear end, he grabbed his spear and pulled it out. As soon as he had the spear clutched firmly in his hand, Paaliaq let the tail go. The bear turned and faced him, full of fury, ready to strike with its huge paws. With all the strength he could muster, Paaliaq thrust his spear into the bear's chest, through its tough skin, just to the left of its breastbone, deep into its lung. He hung on to his spear to keep out of the bear's reach until the bear fell at his feet, dead.

Paaliaq did not brag about this incident. He had not even mentioned it to anyone. But two hunters had happened upon him when he was busy with the bear. They had seen it all. They could not believe what they saw and spread the story far and wide.

There was bear meat for everyone at Paaliaq's camp for a while that winter. Now, many years later, Paaliaq still wore the bearskin short-pants his mother had made for him. He was still a bit fat, very fast, and strong as a bear. Nobody messed with Paaliaq, even though he was sometimes a bit short-tempered.

Paaliaq was a good shaman. But, even shamans have bad days. And, as we will soon see, sometimes it is not such a good time to have a bad day. Today would be one of those days.

Travelling

The-man-with-no-eyebrows urged his dogs on as they pulled his family south. They travelled on the sea ice, along the west coast of the big bay called Tariuq (Salt). During the day, the snow on the ice softened. The sled did not glide well on soft snow, wanting instead to stick to it. To keep the sled from sticking, you had to keep it moving. So The-man-with-no-eyebrows kept it going. He had tied a piece of sealskin line to the sled and was helping his dogs pull, the leather thong stretched over his right shoulder and around his chest. He guided the sled with his left hand.

"Hut, hut!" he urged his dogs on as he pulled. "Auva ih, uai!"

He continually gave his lead dog instructions in a special language he always used with his team, just as his father had taught him, long ago. His lead dogs were always females. They were smarter and easier to train than the big, strong males. And the big males would follow them everywhere. That, too, his father had taught him.

Usually, Can't-see helped when the snow was soft and the going was tough. Everybody had a job to do and she did not like to be a burden. She would walk ahead of the dogs, urging them on, showing them the way. But now, she sat on the sled, carrying Wolverine on her back. The-man-with-no-eyebrows would not let her help today. He had not let her help the day before that, either. He wanted her to take care of their baby. He insisted she sit, like a pampered child, on the sled. She was embarrassed about it and was glad there was no one else around to see her sitting there, on the sled, when the going was so hard. But her husband was very happy. He said that, today, he would do all the work. He strained on his line with tireless determination. There was a flicker in his eyes. He looked like he could run all the way.

Even the dogs seemed to be in a good mood. They strained on their harnesses, pulling hard like they did when they were returning home from a long hunting trip and knew days of rest were coming.

The-man-with-no-eyebrows was glad the snow had not yet completely melted from the top of the ice. When there was bare ice, the dogs' paws turned raw and bled. He had to make little bootees for them with holes for their long nails to stick out of. The bootees kept the hard ice from cutting the soft pads on the bottoms of their paws, but the dogs found them uncomfortable and tended to chew them off. But now, there was no need for bootees.

They had crossed the treacherous ice at the mouth of the long inlet, just south of Big Rapids, the morning before, before the snow softened in the lengthening daylight. And, in the soft snow of the long afternoon, the sled was harder to pull. But The-man-with-no-eyebrows did not mind. He strained on his line and urged his dogs on. A light breeze blew from the west again today. The air smelled of bare ground. Yes, spring was in the air.

In late afternoon, the small family approached Bit-of-sand. The shadows over the uqalurat (the tongues of snow created by the north winds of winter) were long. The uqalurat looked like outstretched tongues trying to catch snowflakes, their tips pointing north. The-man-with-no-eyebrows was tired after pulling his sled all day, but he was happy at the prospect of seeing other people and showing off his new son. Looking south, his keen eyes made out one lone igloo with two people standing beside it. He squinted, trying to get a sharper view in the distance.

"Paaliaq," he said to his wife.

"Ii," Can't-see replied. "Yes."

In this sparse land, there aren't many people who don't know one another.

"Alianait!" The-man-with-no-eyebrows exclaimed and leaned into his piece of rope. "This is wonderful. I did not expect to see anyone so soon."

He puckered up his lips and gave a shrill whistle. His dogs, too, leaned on their harnesses.

A Curse Is Uttered

It had been a long and idle day at Bit-of-sand, as days are when the coldest part of winter has passed. The sun had slowly travelled to the centre of the sky. It had made its lazy way west and stuck to the earth. As it reluctantly sank below the horizon, Paaliaq's dogs barked, announcing the approach of a travelling party. Paaliaq gave his crying baby to his wife and went outside. His mother joined him, and together, they watched the small family making its way over the snow.

When they were close enough to recognize, Paaliaq said, "It is The-man-with-no-eyebrows. He seems to be pulling his wife."

"Yes," his mother replied. "I wonder if there is something wrong."

They peered intently at the travellers, their brows furrowed, trying to make out every detail. But they were still too far away.

Paaliaq said, "We should get some food ready. They will be hungry."

"Yes, I was thinking that," his mother said. "I will go in and start preparing food."

She went back into the igloo. Paaliaq stayed outside and waited.

The travellers meandered left and right, as travellers will, keeping to level ground as much as they could, disappearing behind huge piles of ice and snow now and again. At long last, they arrived, and smiling, shook hands with Paaliaq—well, not so much shaking hands as touching—as if they were making sure Paaliaq was real. They had not seen each other, or anyone else, in a very long time.

Finally, having established they were not dreaming, The-man-with-no-eyebrows said, "Let me introduce you to my son."

He lifted the hood of his wife's amaut, a special baby-carrying coat worn mostly by women. In the pouch at the back, under the hood, Wolverine was fast asleep, warm and snug.

"This is Wolverine," The-man-with-no-eyebrows said proudly.

"Ataatakuluit?" Paaliaq asked, tenderly touching the

little boy on his cheek with the back of his hand. "Your little father?"

"Yes," The-man-with-no-eyebrows said.

"Born only the-day-before-yesterday-plus-one-before-that," Can't-see said, which, of course, is how Inuit say "three days ago."

"Itiritti," Paaliaq said. "Come inside."

They entered the igloo. On the left side of the sleeping platform sat Paaliaq's wife, Auk. She held a baby in a caribou-skin bunting bag. Paaliaq's mother was busily preparing food for their guests. Paaliaq sat down beside his wife.

"Alianairaannuk; tikittuannuuvisii?" Auk said. "What happiness; you have arrived?"

"Ii—yes," Can't-see said. They shook hands with Auk and Paaliaq's mother.

Holding his head high with a great proud look and a satisfied smile on his face, Paaliaq reached for the baby on his wife's lap.

"This is Breath," he said.

As soon as he picked her up, Breath began to cry. And, immediately, Paaliaq's face changed. It was like he had put a mask on. He had the uncomfortable look of someone who is not used to having babies crying on his lap. He began to bounce Breath up and down, trying to get her to stop. Breath cried louder. Frustration showed on Paaliaq's face.

Still a bit short-tempered, The-man-with-no-eyebrows thought, a twinkle in his eye.

Trying hard not to show his anger, Paaliaq held his baby girl, bouncing her up and down. She cried louder, and the louder she cried, the harder he bounced her. And, the harder he bounced her, the louder she cried.

"A beautiful girl," Can't-see said over the din.

"Yes," Paaliaq beamed, forgetting his anger for a moment.

Hinting to her husband, Can't-see said, "So cute!" a little louder.

Paaliaq smiled from ear to ear.

"Let me take her," Can't-see said.

Paaliaq handed her the baby. Immediately, Breath stopped crying. Paaliaq suddenly remembered his anger. His smile disappeared. His eyes narrowed. A frown appeared on his brow. *My daughter cries when I hold her and stops when someone else picks her up*, he thought. *Disgraceful!*

"Yes, she is a beautiful girl," Can't-see said a little too loudly, looking at her husband, trying to get his attention.

Paaliaq turned to The-man-with-no-eyebrows. The-man-with-no-eyebrows was looking casually at him, his eyes bright with amusement. *He is laughing at me*, Paaliaq thought. *He thinks I am short-tempered*. This thought made Paaliaq even angrier. His face turned red with rage.

"Urm, urm!" Can't-see cleared her throat loudly, look-ing straight at her husband.

The-man-with-no-eyebrows turned to his wife. She was not looking amused. As a matter of fact, she was looking downright angry, angry at her husband who was not paying attention. He was having too good a time, laughing at the short-tempered Paaliaq. But finally, she had gotten his attention. She looked down at the baby she was holding in her arms. She looked back at her husband and cocked her head toward Paaliaq and his family. At last, The-man-with-no-eyebrows got the hint. And looking like a sorry dog, he nodded.

Can't-see handed the baby girl back to Paaliaq. Breath started to cry with new vigour, practising her voice with all her might. Paaliaq bounced her up and down, a little too much for the baby girl. He stood up, still bouncing his baby up and down, up and down.

It was a bad time to cry; it was a bad time to be angry; it was a bad time to ask a question, but Can't-see had made a suggestion. The-man-with-no-eyebrows now understood what his wife wanted. This girl would be Wolverine's wife-to-be. He composed himself, put on as serious a face as he could muster, and posed the question over Breath's cries:

"Can we arrange for her to marry my son when they become of age?" he said.

It was a perfectly good question, of course. That

was the way you became engaged to marry someone. When you were born, your parents arranged it all for you. All you had to do was to grow up, and when you were ready, you went to pick up your wife. That was all there was to it. That was the way The-man-with-no-eyebrows had married his wife. That was the way Paaliaq had married his. Their parents had arranged it all for them when they were born. They were a little shy at first, but they got used to it. And they grew to love each other.

But Paaliaq was short-tempered. And now he was mad, and he was not thinking very clearly. He just said things that came into his mouth for no reason at all. And when one is angry, what comes into one's mouth is usually a disagreement. That is what came into Paaliaq's mouth and that is what came out.

He said, "No!"

No? The-man-with-no-eyebrows was surprised at the answer to his question, and the way it was given. He started to say, "But why . . ."

But Breath cried louder. Paaliaq, no longer just bouncing his baby, was now jumping up and down. He grew angrier and angrier. He interrupted The-man-with-no-eyebrows and repeated, "No!!"

Everyone looked at him, bafflement in their eyes. But there was no turning back now. Paaliaq fumed. He did not know why he had said "No" but it was said, and the only thing to do was to stick with what he'd said. He thought what else he might add by way of explanation but something else came into his mouth and he said it before he had time to think about it.

He said, "As a matter of fact, when your son is of age to marry, he will never set foot on this land again!"

He said this, holding his crying daughter firmly in his left arm, his right arm and forefinger pointing down beneath his feet, jumping up and down all the while, looking like he was poking his finger at the ground.

And all of a sudden, everything stopped. Breath stopped in mid-cry. Paaliaq stopped jumping up and down, his right forefinger still pointing straight down at the ground beneath his feet. Everyone seemed to be holding their breath. No one moved. It was completely silent in the igloo. A curse had been uttered. The-man-with-no-eyebrows had heard it clearly. Can't-see had heard it. Auk and Paaliaq's mother had heard it. Everyone had heard it.

They all looked at Paaliaq, eyes wide and mouths open. No one understood what he had meant by what he had said or why he had said it. Even Paaliaq was not sure what he had meant by his own words. But Breath was his daughter, and as humble a dwelling as it was, this was his igloo. He had built it with his own hands. He could say whatever he wanted to say in it. He did not take his words back.

Introducing Mr. Siksik

Outside, a pair of beady eyes looked steadily at the gentle glow of the igloo and the shadows of the occupants within, cast by the light of the seal-oil lamp against the round walls. It was cold outside now, and the animal behind the eyes shivered. His ugly face scowled with interest. He, too, had heard the curse and he knew exactly what the words meant. He had been with Paaliaq a long time. He understood the shaman perfectly, whether he was being bad-tempered or not. The creature was the one who would work the spell; he would make the boy "never set foot on this land again." He made Paaliaq's curses work, good or bad. This was a bad one, and the bad ones were his most favourite curses of all. All he had to do now was to wait until the time was right. He could wait. He was a patient creature. He rubbed his paws together in anticipation. A curse on a baby boy, now that was a joy. He could dance. He forgot all about the cold night air. The only sign of the cold now was in his eyes. They glittered like the stars just starting to appear way above him.

How would he handle this curse? The baby would grow to become a young boy. The boy would grow to become a young man. The young man would eventually become a man, a man old enough to marry. And then, the creature told himself, he would make it happen. There was time. He had time to think about it. But already, a plan began to form in his tiny brain. Yes, he would enjoy this curse. And he had many years to plan it. Oh, what happiness.

The-Man-with-No-Eyebrows

Inside, things had gone back to normal, more or less. Paaliaq had given Breath back to his wife. Paaliaq's mother had begun to dish out some food, saying, "Nirigitti—eat!"

The-man-with-no-eyebrows was not happy about the answer he had received and was puzzled by it. But he tried not to show his disappointment. He had received an answer and the answer was "No." That was all there was to it. There was nothing more to be done about that. He, too, was patient. Paaliaq had spoken, and questioning him would only provoke a confrontation. And one did not confront Paaliaq offhandedly.

There was no point in trying to find a wife for his son now. He did not know where Wolverine would be when he was ready to marry. Wherever it was, it would not be "on this land." There was nothing else to do inside Paaliaq's igloo. And he still had to build a shelter for himself and his family before his day was done.

He said, "I must build an igloo."

He turned away from Paaliaq and the others. He crouched down and crawled out the low entranceway. Outside, it was cool, clear, and peaceful.

The-man-with-no-eyebrows stretched his arms out and looked at the darkening sky. *Why do these things happen?* he thought to himself. *Why do people get angry and say bad things?* He wondered about these things, but no answer came. Off to his left, he noticed something walking away. He looked at it, concentrating, trying to see better in the waning light. It was a siksik, walking on the snow.

A siksik is an Arctic ground squirrel. It grows to about a foot and a half, including its long, bushy tail. It is like a prairie dog or a groundhog. This one was young, but already it showed signs of age. It walked on the snow leaving scratchy little tracks with its tiny, slender feet. It stopped at a safe distance and stared intently at Paaliaq's igloo.

The-man-with-no-eyebrows thought, *That's interesting. Why is that siksik walking on the snow? It should be in its hole in the ground sleeping or something, doing whatever it is siksiks do in their holes all winter long.* It was still winter after all. Other siksiks had not yet reappeared above ground.

The-man-with-no-eyebrows walked over to his sled and sat down. He thought about the siksik. *Why was that siksik wandering around in winter? Why was it staring at Paaliaq's igloo with its intense, beady eyes?* And then he remembered what Paaliaq had said in his anger. The-man-with-no-eyebrows understood. A dread came over him.

Paaliaq is a shaman, he thought. *And a shaman has to get his powers from somewhere.* Actually that somewhere was a something, a something called a tuurnngaq—a spirit represented by an animal. Usually, it was a bur-rowing animal: a weasel, a lemming, or a siksik. Paaliaq could conjure up his spirit, his tuurnngaq, which was embodied in this animal, whenever he had a question he, himself, could not answer. The-man-with-no-eyebrows realized this siksik was a very powerful animal. This was Paaliaq's magic animal. Whatever spell Paaliaq wanted to cast, this animal would figure out how to make it work. This animal made the magic happen. Wherever Paaliaq went, this animal followed, waiting for his mas-ter's call. That was why it was out here in the snow now. It had not slept in a warm burrow this winter. It would never sleep in a warm hole in the ground. It would fol-low Paaliaq in summer and winter, in rain and in snow, all year long. It would follow Paaliaq year after year, for many years, until it got old and died. With its death, Paaliaq's powers would die, until he recruited another animal in which to manifest his tuurnngaq.

The-man-with-no-eyebrows shivered. The siksik climbed a piece of ice and stared at him. It looked at his dogs, lying in the snow, resting after a hard and long day. The siksik seemed very serious for such a young animal. It was not playful like a young siksik should be. It seemed to be studying him and his dogs. The-man-with-no-eyebrows wondered why.

My son, my baby has been cursed, he reasoned. *This animal is studying us, to remember us, so it can work its evil magic on us.* With a flush of anger, The-man-with-no-eyebrows reached down and picked up a piece of snow to throw at the wretched thing. But before he stood up again, the siksik had climbed down from its perch and disappeared into the snow. Its day was done; there would be no more curses tonight.

The-man-with-no-eyebrows threw the snow where the siksik had been, anyway. It bounced off the piece of ice the siksik had been sitting on. That made him feel a little better. He had a good aim.

Ajurnarmat, he thought. *There is nothing to be done.* He had a family. He sighed a sigh of love. He had two people to provide for: a woman he had learned to love and his baby boy. He would provide for them as best he could. He was, after all, an angut—a catcher of animals, a hunter, a man. The-man-with-no-eyebrows felt a new sense of responsibility. His family would survive. Nothing would ever come between them.

Building an Igloo

The-man-with-no-eyebrows took his snow-knife and a long, thin, straightened piece of caribou antler from his sled, and set about looking for the right kind of snow with which to build his igloo. He walked around, poking his stick deep into the snow beneath his feet, testing it for hardness, uniformity, and depth. He wanted snow that was not so hard that it would be brittle, and not so soft that it would crumble when he cut it. The snow had to be consistent all the way through to the bottom, not snow that had fallen in layers. Otherwise, his snow blocks would break at the different layers. It could not be too deep, or the igloo would be cold and hard to heat.

When The-man-with-no-eyebrows had found his new building site, he drew a circle in the snow with his stick. The circle would be the size of his new igloo.

He made sure there would be enough room for himself, his wife, and his newborn son. The thought of building an igloo for three made him smile. The siksik and the curse were forgotten for now. He went into the circle and began cutting blocks of snow for the walls.

Presently, Paaliaq came out of his igloo. He looked much calmer than the last time The-man-with-no-eyebrows had seen him. Paaliaq looked up at the sky. A quarter moon had risen and stars twinkled in the roof of the sky. A few trails of creamy white northern lights fluttered beneath them. There was no wind. He looked in the direction where the siksik had burrowed into the snow. There was nothing to be seen. It was dark.

He went back inside and soon came out again. In one hand, he carried a spluttering tallow candle made from the knee-bone of a caribou. In his other hand, he carried a snow-knife. Shielding the candle with the hand that held the snow-knife, he walked over to where The-man-with-no-eyebrows was building the circular walls of his igloo.

The-man-with-no-eyebrows trimmed the blocks with his snow-knife and tapped them into place. Paaliaq cut a little indentation into the snow where The-man-with-no-eyebrows had been cutting his blocks. He laid the candle in the hole and placed a thin layer of snow in front of it, completely enclosing the candle in a cave of snow. He scraped the snow cover with his snow-knife until it was wafer thin. The candle cast a warm glow over the building site. Having produced the light, Paaliaq set to work, cutting more blocks.

He licked the thin, caribou-antler blade of his knife from handle to tip. He turned the blade over and licked the other side. His saliva froze on the blade. The thin layer of ice would allow the knife to cut smoothly into the snow. Holding his knife in both hands, he slit the wall of snow, starting from the surface straight down to the floor, making a number of passes to ensure he had a good groove. About two feet to one side of that, he cut another groove. He cut along the bottom, reaching as far as he could with the blade of his knife. Along the back, about five inches in, he made his final cut, passing his knife back and forth, cutting deeper and deeper, until he reached bottom. He stuck his knife down the back cut and tapped lightly. The block came out nice and even. It was two feet wide, about a foot and a half high, and five inches thick. He handed it to The-man-with-no-eyebrows and started cutting another block.

The two men worked in silence. Paaliaq cut the blocks and handed them to The-man-with-no-eyebrows. The-man-with-no-eyebrows put the blocks up on the wall like bricks, trimmed them, and tapped them into place. There was the sound of snow-knives slicing back and forth, *swish, swish, scrape, scrape* . . . . The igloo went up in a spiral, right to left, curving inward, closing in at the top.

After a time, Paaliaq said, "It should be a nice day tomorrow."

"Yes," The-man-with-no-eyebrows agreed, "a good day to go out for young seals."

"Yes, we will go out there on the ice," Paaliaq replied.

Nothing more was said about the babies. Nothing more was said about the curse. Soon, The-man-with-no-eyebrows placed the last block of snow on the roof, trimmed it, and let it drop into place.

They went outside, filled in all the cracks with more snow, and shovelled snow up the sides. The igloo was done. Barely an hour had passed since the curse was uttered. Tomorrow, The-man-with-no-eyebrows would add a porch, but tonight, they had shelter.

"Qujannamiik," The-man-with-no-eyebrows said to Paaliaq. "Thank you."

Paaliaq said nothing. There was nothing to say. The-man-with-no-eyebrows would have done the same for him. There was no need for a thank-you; it was only a courtesy. In this harsh land, sharing came easily to the people. They shared the work and the catch. The only things that were yours were yourself and your thoughts, your family, and the hunting tools you made yourself. Everything else, you shared. A greedy man did not survive long.

Paaliaq went home. The-man-with-no-eyebrows went back inside the igloo to fix up the sleeping area, the cooking platform, and the working area. Then he fetched everything from his sled. He brought in bedding, the qulliq, and the food. His hunting gear, he left outside. While he was tending to his dogs, Can't-see came out of Paaliaq's igloo and entered their new home.

When he had finished his chores, The-man-with-no-eyebrows followed his wife into their igloo. She had lit the qulliq with the flame from the candle and had made up the bed.

"You need to eat," she said.

She gave him hot, steaming food she had brought from Paaliaq's igloo. The-man-with-no-eyebrows ate ravenously. He had not eaten since noon, when they had stopped briefly in their travels for lunch. When he had finished eating, he held his son for a long time, admiring his face and his tiny hands. Then he went to bed. Before long, he was snoring lightly, dreaming of all the things he would do with his new boy. Can't-see smiled at her sleeping husband. He was a giant of a man but gentle as an eider duck with its eggs.

A Growing Boy

There is a song that goes:

> *Angijuuliruma ataataakkukani*
> *piqatauqattalaarama,*
> *Mikijuunimnili anaanaakkukani*
> *piqatauqattarniaqtunga.*

> *When I am big*
> *I will go with my father,*
> *Now I am small*
> *I will stay with my mother.*

The first memory that Wolverine had of his childhood was that of travelling on the sea ice just south of a place called Tikirarjuaq—Long-forefinger. Long-forefinger is that narrow stretch of land that points southeast into Hudson Bay, south of Marble Island. Wolverine was at the back end of the sled, behind his mother and father. He was lying on his stomach, facing backwards, looking down between the naput—the crosspieces on the sled. He was mesmerized by the dog tracks going by. He could see them through the naput. The creaking of the sled as it glided over the snowdrifts and the *pock, pock, pock, pock* . . . of the dogs' paws breaking through the thin crust of ice on the soft snow made him sleepy. The dogs seemed to be pulling effortlessly.

Now and then, he looked up and around him. It was a beautiful day. The sun was high up in the clear, blue sky. The brightness sparkled on the pristine white ice and snow. It was so bright he had to squint to see clearly. The snow was flat for miles and miles, as far as he could see. Here and there, he saw piles of ice, pushed up on reefs by the tides. The clear ice was a beautiful, bluish green colour.

His mother sat behind him on the sled, her long black hair hanging in two braids down either side of her head. His father wore tan-coloured goggles with thin slits over his eyes. The-man-with-no-eyebrows sat at the forward end of the sled, his legs dangling over the side, his long sealskin whip trailing along the snow, snaking in the tracks behind the sled. Now and then, he would jump off the sled, run forward, and crack his whip over the heads of his dogs, yelling, "Auva ih! Auva ih!!" telling his dogs to turn right in that special language he used with them. When the sled was travelling in a straight line again, he would stop running, wait for the sled to catch up, and sit back down again.

In a sort of daze, Wolverine must have nodded off, because the next thing he remembered, they were arriving at a camp. A wind had picked up, and now there was snow blowing along the ground. It was cold and getting dark.

Wolverine felt the cold in his sleepy body. His mother carried him into an igloo and there was his grandmother, his mother's mother. She was the dearest person he knew. His grandmother and grandfather had come from the big island to the east, just to visit him. She took him from his mother and said, "Irngutakuluuk!—My-little-grandson." That was all she ever called him: My-little-grandson.

"You are cold," she said, taking his outer clothing off. "Do you need to pee?"

"Yes," Wolverine said.

She dug a hole in the floor of her igloo, down by the doorway. "Pee here," she said. "You will get warmer."

Wolverine peed in the hole, and before long, he could feel warmth seeping back into his body. His grandmother was a very wise person; she knew how to make him warm. He ate steaming seal meat with rich broth, lying in his grandmother's furry bed. And before long, he was warm all over. With his grandmother telling him stories, he was soon fast asleep again.

When he woke up the next morning, Wolverine went outside. There were igloos everywhere, more than he had ever seen all in one place, as many as his fingers on both hands. It was a whole community. There were dogs everywhere. There were many people, mostly women and kids. Most of the men were already out hunting seals. Wolverine and his family had spent the night in his grandmother's igloo, but his father was now building one for them—a big one, with a porch. They would be here for a while.

Out there on the sea ice, Wolverine became aware of the world around him. They did not live on the sinaa—the edge of the ice. The sinaa, or floe edge, as it is normally called, is a very dangerous place to be. Sometimes, huge pans of ice broke off, floated away to the open sea, and broke up into little pieces. They did not want to be on that ice when it floated away, so they camped a safe distance away, toward the mainland, but still on the sea ice. Only the hunters ventured out to the floe edge, always careful not to get caught on ice floes. They hunted seals, walruses, whales, polar bears, and other animals to feed themselves and their dogs. Wolverine's father and the other men went out to the mysterious floe edge every day. Every evening, they came back, pulling their catch along the ice and snow behind them.

Wolverine stayed close to the igloos and played with the other children. When there were many kids to play with, they played tag and aattaujaq—toss-and-catch. Tag was like any other game of tag except for the *lands*. These were places you picked and, as soon as you touched them, you could no longer be tagged. They could be a mound of snow, someone's igloo, a sled, or anything else. You ran from someone who was *It*. You ran to land. As soon as It started chasing someone else, you ran to another land, teasing and taunting It all the way. They played tag all day long.

Toss-and-catch was played with a small sack full of fine sand. The game required two teams and plenty of running around. When you had the sack, you threw it to another member of your team before someone from the other team caught you with it. There was never any time to rest. Wolverine had plenty of energy. But he was not used to this game-playing and laughing and teasing and taunting. He had spent so much time by himself. But he discovered he liked the company. He learned joy he had never known. He learned that you could laugh until your stomach hurt.

When the men came back, there was much work to be done. There was the catch to distribute among the people in their camp. There were dogs to feed, hunting implements to be repaired, and clothes to be mended. Wolverine ran from igloo to igloo, carrying meat to people for their cooking pots. He helped feed the dogs. No one was idle.

After the chores were done and they had all eaten, there were stories about the hunt. Wolverine sat in rapt attention as his father raised his right fist. He brought it down suddenly, in a harpooning motion, laughing all the while.

"There was a seal down there," he said. "I harpooned it through the snow cover. I could feel the harpoon go in. But I had no idea what I had harpooned."

In mid-winter, the sea ice is six feet thick. Seals will keep a hole open all winter long, constantly gnawing at the ice with their sharp teeth to keep the hole about two feet wide. Through this hole, the seal will come up for air and then return to the depths below to fish.

The-man-with-no-eyebrows had harpooned what he thought was a common ringed seal. But then it had yanked him down suddenly, headfirst, onto the ice. The harpoon line tied to his wrist stung, and he thought he had broken his wrist. But the line slackened for a moment and he could feel life seeping back into his hand. He had started to pull the line up again, when again, the thing pulled him down with such force, he had fallen and scrunched his face into the snow. By the time the line slackened again his fellow hunters had arrived, running. One of them helped him pull on the line while another cleared the hole of snow and ice with

The-man-with-no-eyebrows' snow-knife. It had taken three full-grown hunters to pull the thing out of the seal hole. What The-man-with-no-eyebrows had caught was the biggest ugjuk—bearded, or square-flipper, seal—they had ever seen. It was much longer than Wolverine's father was tall, and he was the biggest man there.

The-man-with-no-eyebrows scrunched the side of his face with his hand to show how the seal had pulled him down onto the ice, and laughed and laughed as he told the story. His wrist was still sore.

Wolverine listened to this story and others and looked forward to growing up. He looked forward to the days when he would go hunting with his father. But for now, he was too little. He stayed in the community of igloos and played with the other kids. Every evening, he helped the men when they returned from the flow edge.

He spent most nights in his grandmother's igloo. She spoiled him as grandparents are wont to do. They played many games. His grandparents told many wonderful stories to put him to sleep. Wolverine decided they would live like that forever.

But there are times of plenty and there are lean times. As winter wore on and the coldest days of the year drew near, the men returned from the floe edge with fewer and fewer seals. There was less meat to distribute among the villagers. The dogs were getting snarly. Like the people in the village, they, too, were eating less and less. And for Wolverine, the stories of the hunt became stories of waiting and waiting, forever waiting for the seals that refused to surface to breathe.

The Old Woman under the Sea

Sometimes, life is not cozy at all. With a stiff offshore wind, a giant piece of ice breaks off the floe edge. That piece of ice floats out to sea. It breaks up into little pieces and finally reverts to its basic element: water. There is water as far as the eye can see. And one day, the wind calms. What was the edge of the ice yesterday—with ducks and seals that fish close to the surface of the water—freezes over. A thin layer of ice, too thin to walk on, covers miles and miles of ocean. Winter bites hard like an angry, frightened wolverine and refuses to let go. The winds blow and blow. Snow drifts along the surface of the ice in an ethereal flow, weaving over and under itself like long strands of white yarn, ever twisting, never getting themselves entangled, forever blowing, drifting, over and under, for miles and miles and miles.

The hunters went out every day. The new ice stretched on, as far as they could see. The-man-with-no-eyebrows could see ripples in it, caused by the waves and the currents underneath. Where he wanted to be was at the edge of that ice, where seals come up in the open sea. But he was not sure enough to walk on the new ice. He stepped on it with his dogs, and immediately, the dogs began to crouch, their legs shaking. They were scared to walk on it; they could feel it move. The-man-with-no-eyebrows stepped back and got on the solid ice again. He, too, finally had to hunker down and wait for the ice to thicken.

But, as he waited, he still had to eat. He had to feed his family. He had to feed his dogs because he depended on them for his very survival. He tried the seal holes. But the elusive seals, in their mysterious refuge down below the ice, refused to come up to breathe in their holes. There was nothing left. If they stayed, they would slowly eat up all their food. They would burn up all the seal fat that they needed to warm their igloos.

One by one, the families packed their belongings and left, looking for better places to hunt. Some travelled north; some travelled south, hoping to find a place where the floe edge was closer and less dangerous. Some travelled inland to look for caribou, Arctic hare, and ptarmigan, and to fish in the freshwater lakes.

And, one day, Wolverine's grandfather took him by his shoulders, looked into his eyes, and said, "I have to take your grandmother away for a while. We have to go home before spring comes."

Wolverine said, "Do you really have to go?"

"Yes," his grandfather said. "Your aunts and uncles and your cousins are waiting for us at Farther-out-to-sea. We have to be with them, too. But I will bring your grandmother back."

Wolverine hugged his grandmother and cried for a long time. His grandparents left. They travelled north, heading for the strait where they would cross over to the big island called Farther-out-to-sea. Wolverine watched them until they disappeared in the distance.

The-man-with-no-eyebrows and his family were the only ones left in their lonely camp, surrounded by cold, abandoned igloos with open, dark, gaping entrance-ways; a ghost town, way out there on the sea ice. He, too, could go inland, of course, but one took chances. When it came to a choice of trying one's luck out on the sea ice or up on land, The-man-with-no-eyebrows preferred to take his chances on the sea ice. It had never let him down before. So the small family stayed.

Every day The-man-with-no-eyebrows walked along the sea ice with two of his best sniffing dogs. The dogs strained on their harnesses, their noses to the snow. They sniffed like wolves, moving here and there. Every now and then they stopped at a promising spot and sniffed all around. Then they moved on. The scent was weak. The hole had been abandoned for too long. When the dogs finally found a hole with a fresh scent, The-man-with-no-eyebrows poked a small opening in the snow cover. He took a long, thin, curved piece of caribou antler, carefully fed it into the small hole, and felt around the walls of the seal hole underneath to determine exactly where it was. Carefully, he peeled off a single strand of white eiderdown from a piece of eider duck skin and, with his saliva, stuck it to a small, three-pronged holder. Once it was frozen in place, he carefully placed the point of the eiderdown holder in the small hole in the snow. He attached the harpoon head to his harpoon. And then he crouched down and watched the strand of eiderdown attached to its holder, waiting for any movement it might make.

When the sun appears in late morning and sets in mid-afternoon, when the snows drift over the tundra plains and Hudson Bay has been frozen over for a very long time, it gets awfully cold out there on the sea ice. The sea ice is the coldest place in this world. There is no shelter from the winds, just you and hundreds of miles of ice and snow and cold, damp sea air that blows into every little hole in your clothes. The-man-with-no-eyebrows wore two caribou-skin coats, the inside one with the fur on the inside, the outside one with the fur on the outside. He watched that small strand of white eider-down. It would move if the air under the snow was dis-turbed, if a seal came up the hole to breathe. But it did not move, no matter how long he watched it. He waited and waited, and as he waited, many questions began to play on his mind: What were the seals doing while they were refusing to come up to breathe? They had to come up for air sometime. What were they up to? Did they not like him? Did he do something to offend them in some way? What was it like down there anyway? *There is something wrong,* he thought, *terribly wrong.*

Can't-see was beginning to worry, too. She was the keeper of the stores of food and fat, and they were get-ting dangerously low. One day, she said to her husband, "We should go somewhere else."

"Yes," The-man-with-no-eyebrows replied. "I suppose we have to go. I think we should go and find Paaliaq. He might be at Bit-of-sand. We will head that way. He is the only person who can help us now."

"What if Paaliaq is not at Bit-of-sand?" Can't-see asked.

The-man-with-no-eyebrows said, "Then we will travel farther north. I have a caribou cache close to Big Rapids. It should take us no more than five days to get there."

Can't-see said, "I will start packing."

And so it was that The-man-with-no-eyebrows and Can't-see set out to find their reluctant friend Paaliaq, the short-tempered shaman. They travelled north, past Long-forefinger. They stopped briefly at The-land-of-young-caribou to look for caribou. But The-land-of-young-caribou was not living up to its name. There was not a caribou to be seen anywhere. They travelled over The-land-of-the-bull-caribou, a long point of land just south of A-small-inlet. The-land-of-the-bull-caribou, too, was not living up to its name. They travelled through the Big Islands and across A-small-inlet and to Bit-of-sand. There was one igloo at Bit-of-Sand.

It was then they greeted each other and Auk said, "Tikittuannuuvisii? Alianairaannuk—You have arrived? What happiness." The-man-with-no-eyebrows and Can't-see shared a feast with what little food they had, and Breath and Wolverine played.

After this meagre feast, the reason for the visit was discussed. How could a man of The-man-with-no-eyebrows' skill and patience have trouble feeding his family? The-man-with-no-eyebrows did not know. Perhaps he had neglected to share? No, The-man-with-no-eyebrows would never forget to be generous. He would share his last scrap of food with anyone. Perhaps he had not treated his catches with the respect they deserved, not given them their last fresh drink on this earth? They come from very salty waters and have to be given a drink of freshwater before they leave this earth forever, so they may never again be thirsty. But, of course,

The-man-with-no-eyebrows would never neglect to give them a drink when he caught them. Perhaps Nuliajuk is frustrated and angry again?

Well, Paaliaq would go down and speak with Nuliajuk.

The mysterious deep of Hudson Bay is a very fascinating place. In this dark and forbidding place live a multitude of animals: whales, walruses, fishes of all kinds, mussels, crabs, starfish, and tiny shrimp-like creatures called kinguit.

◆◆◆

Also, somewhere down in the watery depths lives a strange old woman. Her name is Nuliajuk. Her name is Sedna. Her name is The-one-down-there. She goes by many names. There are many stories about her. Nobody really knows what the real story about her is because she has lived down there for a very long time. She sits on the ocean floor, her long hair flowing, moving back and forth with the tides and the currents. When you look down into the sea, over the side of a boat in summer, you can see her hair, swaying back and forth, back and forth. Sometimes, as her hair moves with the water, it gets all dishevelled and tangled up. The creatures of the sea get caught in it and, no matter how hard they try, they cannot get out. It would be so nice if old Nuliajuk would run her fingers through her hair and let all those animals out, but alas, Nuliajuk has no fingers.

You see, a long time ago, when she was just a girl, Nuliajuk refused to marry; she would take no man for a husband. It was a cruel world in which she lived. There were no animals to hunt: no caribou, no seals, no whales, no walruses, no fish—nothing. Her family was starving, and they could no longer feed her. If she had married she would have had a husband who would have supported her, but no, she refused to marry anyone.

One day, her family loaded their boat with the few things they had and headed off to another hunting place, hoping for better luck. They left Nuliajuk behind. They could no longer support a woman who refused to take a husband. Well, Nuliajuk did not want to be left behind. She waded into the water and swam out to the boat. She grabbed the gunwales and tried to climb aboard. Her father took his axe and chopped her fingers off to keep her from climbing in. No longer able to hold on to the gunwales of the boat, Nuliajuk slipped down to the depths of the sea. And that is where she lives to this day. Her fingers, too, fell into the sea after her and sank, one by one. And, one by one, they became the animals of the sea. They became seals, whales, walruses, fishes, and all the other sea creatures.

But now, Nuliajuk has no fingers with which to comb her hair, and when her hair is all tangled up, these poor animals get caught in it and cannot get out. They tickle her head and that makes her angry. She shakes her head. She screams and flails her arms about. She makes the water boil until there are big waves. If her hair gets tangled up, there are no animals to hunt, no meat to eat, no sealskin for boots, no whale-meat to feed the dogs. Even if there were animals about, no one could go out to sea to hunt them when Nuliajuk is angry. The winds blow and the water boils white. Some people get hungry and starve to death. Nuliajuk has become the most feared creature in all the land. She has the power of life and death over all the people.

The only people who can calm Nuliajuk are the shamans. Now and then, they dive down to the bottom of the sea. They run their fingers through her hair and make it all neat and tidy. They free the animals. They remove the shrimp and crabs that make her hair itch and make her frustrated and angry. They soothe her and settle her down. And the seas become calm and smooth again. There are seals, walruses, fish, and whales again. And people can go out to hunt, and again, have food to eat.

❖❖❖

Paaliaq stood up. He walked in a circle, slowly. He put the back of his left hand over his eyes, covering them.

His right hand hung at his side, waving back and forth as he walked in a circle. He said, "Pamiuq—tail," quietly at first. He said it over and over again. And then he said it louder and louder, "Pamiuq, pamiuq!!" until he was screaming it. "PAMIUQ, PAMIUQ, PAMIUQ!!" His body shuddered. Then he was quiet. He kept walking in his circle, his eyes covered, his right hand waving slowly by his side, completely oblivious to the world around him.

His body was there, but Paaliaq was far away, way down under the ice, swimming toward Nuliajuk. When he got there, he embraced Nuliajuk. He talked quietly to her and gently moved her hair away from her eyes. He began to straighten her hair. He ran his fingers through her thick, greying, slick hair. He released the seals caught in it. He let the whales, the fish, and the walruses go. He picked the crabs and the kinguit—the little shrimp-like creatures—out of her scalp. He scratched her head. And then, she was calm, almost dreamy, her hair waving slowly in the watery depths. Paaliaq picked out one last crab and headed back.

Inside his igloo, Paaliaq fell in a heap on the floor. The-man-with-no-eyebrows walked over and helped him up.

"Are you all right?" he said.

"It is done," Paaliaq said.

Outside, Mr. Siksik walked over the snow, staggering under what seemed like a very heavy weight, leaving his little scratchy footprints. He crawled into a hole and promptly fell asleep. His job was done for the day. It was exhausting work taking Paaliaq's soul out of his body and guiding it down under the sea ice. It was not a job he enjoyed, doing good work like that. And Paaliaq had done good, not only for The-man-with-no-eyebrows and his family but also for Nuliajuk, that wretched, hairy old woman. Oh, how Mr. Siksik hated old women.

Inside the igloo, The-man-with-no-eyebrows said, "I must go outside and build an igloo," and left. And, taking his snow-knife, Paaliaq soon followed him. Tomorrow, The-man-with-no-eyebrows would go hunting seals again, and this time, he knew his luck would be better.

In-there

When the sea ice was full of huge cracks and holes and became impassable, The-man-with-no-eyebrows' family made the long trek to their summer camping grounds. Seven ukiuqs—winters—had passed in Wolverine's life; Inuit count their age by winters. Wolverine ran this way and that, inspecting every pond, every rock, and every siksik mound along the way. When he tired, his father picked him up and heaved him up onto his pack. His father carried a huge roll of caribou skins wrapped around hunting tools, dried meats and fish, and tent poles. There, his arms and legs draped around the roll on either side of his father's head, Wolverine slept, rocking back and forth to his father's walk as his father carried him and the roll. His mother did not carry him on her back anymore; he was too big. Besides, she had someone else to carry on her back now: Kuluk, Little-loved-one, his baby sister.

The little family walked along the northern coast of the small bay that would someday be known as Rankin Inlet, named after someone no one would ever remember afterward. Now, it was simply called Kangiqliniq—A-small-inlet—a most reasonable name and one not easily forgotten.

Wolverine loved his baby sister. When she was little, he had made up a song for her, the way adults do, a song called an aqaq:

> Piuluammat, nallinnammat
> ajungiluattuutiummat,
> Iniqunattuutiummaat . . .

It was all very silly, really, and very simple, just a song to praise a little sister as you bounced her up and down on your knee:

> So good, so lovely,
> You can do anything
> And you are so cute,
> Oh! What a sister I have . . .

Wolverine always had his sister by his side or on his back, carrying her everywhere he went. He was her constant babysitter. He was her hero.

The family stopped for a time and fished at a river with an ancient stone fishing weir called Aqquugaaqrjuk—Small-crotch—because it looked like the crotch of a person; Inuit names are very descriptive. The weir had not been used since last year's fishing. Some of the rocks had been carefully removed to allow fish to swim upriver and back down again to feed all summer in the huge, deep salt water of Hudson Bay. It would be used again in the fall as it had been used since it was built, so long ago no one remembered when. Wolverine's father speared fish at the mouth of the river. Wolverine's mother filleted and dried the fish they did not eat for later use. Wolverine's father hunted caribou, and his mother dried the meat to keep it from spoiling. Nothing was ever allowed to spoil. There was nothing wasted. His father hunted geese and gathered eggs, and his mother cooked them for the family to eat.

Sometimes, Wolverine hunted with his father. When he got tired, his father carried him on his shoulders. Most of the time, he ran. His father was a very fast walker and Wolverine had to run to keep up. Sometimes, lying on top of a hill, they watched the caribou, and his father told him about the different kinds of caribou grazing in a field below them. He learned about yearlings, about young bulls, calves, and about female caribou. Sometimes they saw a giant bull lying on a hilltop, big antlers silhouetted against the horizon, surveying the countryside around him, always wary.

"That one, we leave until the next time, until we can catch him off guard. That is the one we want. He has good fat and lots of it," his father said.

Wolverine liked to hunt with his father.

They crossed the river and continued on their journey west. A day later, they came to a big river called Fish. A half-day's trek upriver was a lake called In-there. It also had a fishing weir. Here, they made their summer camp.

There were other families at In-there, among them Paaliaq's. The girls played house, clearing spaces around rocks, making beds, cooking platforms, and drying racks. The boys ran here and there, looking for nesting birds. They threw rocks at the swift songbirds, the big birds, and siksiks, as boys will. They waded into the river looking for fish. And more than once that summer, Wolverine had to be rescued from the fast-flowing water by his mother and the other women in the camp. Then, he would have to lie in bed, waiting for his clothes to dry. As soon as his clothes were dry, he was back in the water; Wolverine was always in water.

Sometimes Paaliaq's daughter, Breath, made him pretend he was her husband in her pretend tent. Wolverine hated it, but he pretended to go and fetch water from the river and to collect moss for the campfire. Breath was a bossy girl.

But Wolverine liked Breath. Sometimes they walked for a long time together, exploring here and there. They played hide-and-seek with the other kids in the camp. Sometimes, they waded and swam in the shallow, warm lakes. Wolverine's favourite times were when he and Breath would lie in Breath's grandmother's tent after a long walk, and Breath's grandmother would tell them stories. Wolverine heard these stories over and over again, but never tired of them. He could not remember when he had first heard them. It was as if the stories had always been there.

The Beginning of the Kiviuq Legends

During the brief, warm summer months, Breath's grand-mother lived by herself in a small, caribou-skin tent. But she was never alone. Breath and Wolverine were always with her. One day, Breath and Wolverine were playing on the bedding when Breath's grandmother said, "Come in, come in," to a little girl standing in the doorway.

Paammakuluk was dressed in rags, her beautiful face black with soot, her jet-black hair unkempt. Her parents had died in an accident on the sea ice when she was just a baby. She lived with her grandparents now, who provided for her as best they could. But her grand-father did not hunt much anymore, and her grand-mother's eyes were dim and failing. Paammakuluk was not well fed and someone would have to hand her down some clothes before winter came.

"Don't block the doorway," Grandmother said to Paammakuluk. "Sit here." She patted a spot beside herself.

The little girl came in and sat down.

"Paammakuluk, how you have grown," Grandmother said with a smile in her wrinkled eyes. She loved this little girl.

Paammakuluk smiled.

A light breeze came up from the bay, keeping the mosquitos away. The tent flaps were open wide and Grandmother was enjoying the beautiful weather.

"Grandmother, tell us a story," Breath said.

Grandmother replied, "I have no story to tell."

It was a game they played every time they wanted a story or when Grandmother wanted to settle them down and put them to sleep: a "Grandmother, tell us a story, But I have no story to tell" game.

"Grandmother, please tell us a story," Wolverine implored; everyone called her Grandmother.

"But I have no story to tell," Grandmother said again.

"Grandmother, please . . ." Paammakuluk said.

"OK," Grandmother said. "Just for you. Now settle down, all of you, and I will tell you a story."

They settled down to listen. And Grandmother told them one of Wolverine's very favourite stories.

"The greatest man who has ever lived is called Kiviuq," she started. "Kiviuq was born a long, long time ago—so long ago, it is said, he was the very first person on earth. Now, I don't know how he got to be the first person on earth, because he had a mother." She gave a little chuckle at her own joke, "Heh, heh!"

"But Kiviuq lives still, today, an old man. They say he is so old his body is turning into stone. His cheeks, his chin, and his forehead are all turning black and hard, as hard as stone." She knocked her forehead and cheeks with her knuckles to show how hard Kiviuq's forehead and cheeks were.

"But his heart still beats. Someday, when his heart turns completely into stone and stops, that will be the end of the world."

She patted Paammakuluk's hair with her wrinkled, tattooed hand and continued. "The story of Kiviuq begins this way:

Once there was a little boy, a little boy much like Wolverine here. He was so small and naughty and was forever wading in water, getting himself all wet. I am sure his grandmother kept him in bed, many a day, while she dried his clothes.

Now this little boy was an iliarjuk, an orphan; he had no mother and no father. He only had his grandmother to live with.

Like any little boy, this boy loved to play. So, every day, he would go outside to play. But there were mean boys who lived in his village. They would laugh at the way he dressed. They would laugh at him because he had no one to teach him how to hunt and provide for himself and his grandmother. They would run after him. They would fight him and make him cry. They would tear up all his clothes. The poor boy would go home to his grandmother and his poor old grandmother would take her needle and thread, and she would sew his clothes all back together again.

This boy and his grandmother were poor and they had to make do with what they had. The boy's clothes were made of loon skins. There is nothing wrong with loon skins, of course. We still use them today. But this boy's clothes were old and the skin was brittle. Loon skins make good clothing, but they tear very easily, especially when they are old.

Every day, the boy went out to play, and every day, the mean boys ran after him, fought him, made him cry, and ripped apart all his clothes. And, every day, his poor old grandmother, with her failing eyes and feeble fingers, threaded her needle and sewed his clothes all back together again.

One day, his grandmother decided, "I am tired of all this fighting. I am tired of sewing perfectly good clothes back together again."

And, I guess, she was not unfamiliar with the ways of shamans. She had some strong magical powers of her own and she set about making use of them. When the boy came home, crying, with his clothes ripped to shreds again, there was a little seal that someone had caught for them lying on the floor of their tent. She pointed to the seal and said, "Grandson, I would like you to skin that seal."

The little boy took a knife and began to skin the seal. "Be careful. Be very careful," his grandmother said. "Don't put any holes in the skin."

So, very carefully, the little boy skinned the seal, making sure he did not put any holes in the skin. When he was finished, his grandmother said, "Take the sealskin and pull it over your head so it fits nicely. You should be able to see through the eyeholes. Yes, just like that. Now, put your head in that pail of water and keep your head underwater as long as you can."

There was a big pail of water on the floor. The little boy took a deep breath and stuck his head into the pail of water. He kept his head underwater as long as he could. When his lungs began to hurt, he lifted his head and breathed, taking deep breaths. His grandmother said, "Do it again."

So again, the little boy took a deep breath and

stuck his head into the pail of water. He kept his head underwater as long as he could. When his lungs were just about to burst, he lifted his head again and breathed, gulping air. And again, his grandmother said, "Do it again."

The little boy took another deep breath and stuck his head back into the pail of water. He kept his head underwater as long as he could, and when he was just about to drown, he lifted his head and breathed, gulping air, taking deep breaths, and again, his grandmother said, "Do it again."

Every time he lifted his head, his grandmother would say, "Do it again." The little boy would take a deep breath and stick his head back into the pail of water. He would keep his head underwater as long as he could. After a while, he could keep his head underwater for a long, long time. He would keep his head underwater so long, you could see the sun move before he had to take another breath. It was only then that his grandmother was satisfied: satisfied that her grandson could keep his head underwater long enough.

She said, "Grandson, I would like you to go down to the beach now. When you are walking to the beach, stay low and make sure no one sees you. When you get to the water's edge, pull the sealskin over your head like I taught you and dive into the water. Swim underwater along the shore. When you are directly in front of all your mean friends who are playing on the beach, I want you to come up for air. Do you understand?"

The little boy nodded his head.

"Swim slowly along the beach like you have no worry in the world. They will see you. If they don't, I will say, 'There is a little seal,' and point you out. Do you understand?"

The little boy nodded his head again.

She said, "Go, now. Go and lead them all out to sea."

The little boy took the sealskin and headed down to the sea. He crouched low, making sure no one saw him as he walked. When he was on the beach, he took the sealskin and carefully pulled it down over his head. He made sure it fitted nicely so he looked like a seal. He jumped into the water and swam underwater, along the beach. After a while, he lifted his head above the water and looked toward the beach. Sure enough, there were the mean boys, playing on the beach. He saw one of them point to him and yell, "There's a little seal!"

All the boys ran for their kayaks, picked them up, put them in the water, and hopped in. They shoved off. They took their long paddles and dipped them in the water. The little seal dove underwater and swam out to sea, not too far ahead of the mean boys, just far enough ahead to stay out of the reach of their harpoons. When he came up for air, he saw the boys paddling their kayaks hard, following him. Again, he went down and swam a little farther out. Still the mean boys followed him. He went down and swam farther out, leading the boys out to sea.

It was a beautiful day. The sea was calm; there was not a ripple in the water. Still the little seal went down underwater. He swam a little farther out and surfaced again. And still the mean boys followed. Before long, they were way out at sea. Then, the little seal began to sing every time he surfaced. When he came up for air, he would lift his hands and his legs up to the sky, like a baby lying on its back, and he would sing, *"Anuriga nauk? Anuriga qaili. Ungaa, ungaa . . ."* And then, he would go down underwater again.

When he came up for air again, he would wave his hands and his legs up in the air like a baby wailing and crying and he would sing out, *"Anuriga nauk? Anuriga qaili. Ungaa, ungaa . . ."* And again, he would go down beneath the surface of the water.

When he lifted his head above the water to breathe again, he would lift his hands and his legs and he would sing, "Where is my wind? I want my wind." And he would make a crying sound like a little baby, "Wah, waah!"

They say, the weather that was on the day you were born, is your very own weather. That is why, if you were born on a rainy day, it usually rains on the date of your birth; if you were born on a sunny day, the sun usually shines on your birthday. Well, this little boy was born on a very, very windy day and he was calling the weather of his birth, *"Anuriga nauk? Anuriga qaili. Ungaa, ungaa . . . —Where is my wind? I want my wind. Wah, waah!"*

The wind heard him, and came to him. It came and it came. And with the wind came waves, big waves. Before long, the kayaks were going up and down, up and down with the waves. Every now and then, a big white wave came crashing down on the kayaks and flipped them over. One by one, the mean boys, who fought him and made him cry and ripped apart all his clothes, were sinking to the bottom of the sea. And before long, there were only two kayaks left. Those two kayaks belonged to Kiviuq and his brother.

Now, Kiviuq was a very strong boy and he was very good with a paddle. When a big wave came and flipped his kayak over, he would flip it back up again with his long paddle. His brother would do the same thing; when a big wave came and flipped his kayak over, he would flip it back up with his paddle. But, after a while, Kiviuq's brother got so tired and wet and cold, he could not keep his kayak up anymore. Kiviuq would go over to help him and flip his kayak back up, but then even Kiviuq became so cold and wet and tired, he could not help his brother anymore. His brother's kayak flipped over one last time and he sank to the bottom of the sea. Now there was only one person left. Kiviuq.

Kiviuq paddled his kayak on and on, day and night. No matter how tired he was, he paddled on. No matter how wet and cold he got, he paddled on. When a big wave came and flipped his kayak over, he rolled it back up. He would not give up. Because he could not get up to pee or do anything else, his kayak got very smelly after a while, but he continued on, up and down, up and down, and over and back up again. He kept going. He never, ever gave up.

Finally, after a long time, the wind stopped and the sea became very still again. Kiviuq was so tired, he put his paddle on his lap, his head on his chest, and he fell asleep. He slept, sitting there in his kayak, for a very long time.

When he woke up, Kiviuq looked around; he looked all around, but he saw nothing: nothing but water. Water, water everywhere. He was way out in the middle of the ocean. Because he was way out in the middle of the ocean, he could not see any land anywhere. And, because he could not see any land anywhere, he did not know which way to go.

Ever since he was a little boy, Kiviuq's mother had always sewed a feather on the back of his coat. It was a feather from a little bird called a saurraq—a red-necked phalarope. A saurraq is a brown bird that likes to swim in ponds. When it is swimming, it goes around and around in circles, poking its beak forward, again and again. It is a funny little bird. Kiviuq had always wondered what that feather was for.

While he was sitting there, not knowing which way to go, a bird came, a little white bird, a snow bunting. The bird landed on the bow of his kayak. *What is this?* Kiviuq thought. But the little bird only looked at him and said, "Do you know which way to go?"

Kiviuq said, "No," waving his arms all around him. "I don't know which way to go because there is nothing but water."

The little bird said, "Well, follow me."

Kiviuq dipped his paddle in the water and followed the little bird, sitting there on the bow of his kayak. He paddled his kayak on and on. After a long time, he saw a thin line on the horizon, like a piece of thread. He thought it was land so he paddled his kayak toward it. But after a time, it disappeared.

Kiviuq shrugged his shoulders and said, "It must have been a big wave."

The little bird turned around. It looked up at him and asked again, "Do you know which way to go?"

Again, Kiviuq replied, "No. There is nothing but water."

The little bird said again, "Well, follow me."

And again, Kiviuq followed the little bird, sitting on the bow of his kayak. He paddled his kayak on and on. After a time, he saw a thin line on the horizon, like a thin piece of thread. He paddled his kayak toward it, thinking it must be land. And again, it disappeared.

Kiviuq said, "It must have been a big wave."

The little bird asked him again, "Do you know which way to go?"

For the third time, Kiviuq replied, "No. There is nothing but water."

The little bird said, yet again, "Then, follow me."

Kiviuq followed the little bird, paddling his kayak. After a time, he saw a thin line on the horizon once more. He paddled his kayak toward it, thinking it must surely be land. And this time, the thin line did not disappear. It got thicker and thicker, and Kiviuq landed his kayak, way over on the other side of the ocean, in this strange place where no one had ever been before.

"And that is where that part of the story ends."

◆◆◆

When Grandmother finished the story, Paammakuluk was fast asleep, leaning on Wolverine. Grandmother kissed her on her cheek. Then she said to the other two, "I don't remember whatever happened to that little orphan boy. He swam back home and lived quite happily without all the mean boys, I imagine. Take heed, Wolverine and Breath, always be kind to orphans like Paammakuluk here. They have something very powerful looking out for them."

There was always a moral in the stories Grandmother told. That was the way of the old people. They taught the young morals, morals by which they would grow, morals that would guide them in their lives.

"That was the first story about Kiviuq," she added. "All the rest are stories about how he travelled from that strange land, trying to find his way home."

As he was drifting off to sleep, Wolverine thought,

Someday, I will be like Kiviuq. I will paddle my kayak in big waves, in a big storm, way out at sea. What he did not realize was, that someday, that was exactly what he would do.

Ukpigjuaq, Big Owl

When Wolverine had survived nine winters, his family came back to the lake called In-there, like they did most summers. It was one of those lazy times when it is too early to begin worrying about preparing for winter, when the weather is too warm to gather more food because it will only spoil, when people are fed and happy. One day Wolverine's father said, "I need a new kayak."

Paaliaq said, "I need one, too."

To build their kayaks, they had to make frames and cover them with a waterproof material. That was simple enough. There are plenty of seals in the waters just east of In-there. They had many sealskins with which to cover their kayaks. But, to build the frames, they needed wood. There is no wood at In-there. To get the wood, they had to cut down some trees. The closest trees are three hundred miles away. So they had to walk three hundred miles to get the wood for their kayaks. They gathered tools and provisions and prepared for a long journey.

Wolverine said, "Can I come?"

"No," his father said. "The journey will take many, many days. It is a dangerous journey. We have to go to the place where the trees stand in the ground. The people in the trees are not always friendly. I want you to take good care of your mother and your sister."

Wolverine realized he was not being told to stay because he was too small for such a journey. He had heard of the savage people in the trees, the Unaliit (Fighting-people) and the Iqqiliit (People-with-louse-eggs). They spoke a foreign language and Wolverine's people did not understand them. They had strange ways. When his people and the Iqqiliit met, there was always a fight, and sometimes, people were killed. But his father and Paaliaq needed the wood from the trees to build their kayaks. He was being told to look after his mother and his little sister. He realized, if his father did not return from that dangerous place, someone would have to provide for them. His father was trusting him with that job.

"Yes, Father," he said.

The-man-with-no-eyebrows and Paaliaq crossed the river at the stone weir and left, heading southwest.

In the days and weeks that followed, Wolverine and the other boys in his village hunted small game with their bows and arrows and their spears. They snared Arctic hare and gathered goose eggs. The women and girls gathered roots and sweet leaves, dried meats for winter, and gathered moss for the cooking fires. Now and then, Wolverine and his family walked down to the sea to spear fish in the tidal flats and bring the fish back. There was no shortage of food. Men hunted seals and caribou, and as always, the meat was shared with everyone in the camp.

Wolverine and Breath spent a lot of time together. They walked a great deal. One day, they were walking to a small inlet in the tidal waters where mussels cling to rocks. They would gather the mussels to bring back with them. As they walked, they saw an ukpigjuaq—a big owl, more commonly known in English as a snowy owl—take flight ahead of them. They had seen it before and had taken no notice of it. But a gyrfalcon swooped down and hit the ground close to where the owl had flown from. There was a struggle and they saw white feathers flying. The owl came back and chased the falcon away.

Wolverine and Breath walked to the place where they had seen the struggle taking place. The big owl flew away. As they approached, the big owl swooped down at them over and over again, trying to chase them away.

Holding their hands over their heads, they approached. Eventually, the big owl stopped trying to chase them away. It landed on a rock, a short distance away. They found a nest. And, near the nest, they found a young owl. It was lying on the ground beside the nest, its head resting in an odd way, its left eye looking straight up at them. Wolverine walked around it. The eye followed him. Carefully, he approached, but the owl did not move.

"It's sick," Wolverine said.

"Maybe it's only hurt," Breath said. "I think the falcon thought it was a ptarmigan. They usually don't bother owls, but this one isn't much bigger than a ptarmigan."

Wolverine picked it up. Its right wing was limp. It hung straight down.

Wolverine said, "It has a broken wing."

"You'd better kill it," Breath said. "We can take it home. Owl meat is very good."

The owl kept its eye on Wolverine.

What Breath had said was true; owl meat is very good. But something stopped Wolverine. He could not get himself to kill the bird. The look in the owl's eyes reminded him of Paammakuluk somehow, a look of pleading, a look of helplessness. "Be kind to those who cannot help themselves," he could hear Grandmother saying.

He also felt a sense of power, power over a frail, helpless living thing. He noticed his heart beating hard. The bird was in his hand. All he had to do was to twist its neck and they would have owl meat. And he really had no qualms about killing an animal for food. It was a job he had been given, to provide food for his family when his father was away. But they had plenty of food, and the owl was suffering. He had to make a decision.

He said, "Once, my uncle broke his arm. He was really hurt and would not let anyone touch it. My father had to fight him to try to get some sense into him, and when he finally got tired, my father pulled on his broken arm until it was straight again. He tied sticks to it to keep it straight until it healed. Now his arm is just like it always was. He says it sometimes gets cold, but it is fine. Maybe we can fix this wing."

Breath thought for a minute. "OK," she said, "let's do it."

Wolverine turned to the big owl and yelled, "We'll take care of your baby!"

He was happy. A heavy burden had been lifted from his mind. He had not really wanted to kill the bird. They ran home as fast as they could, Wolverine carrying the owl. The mussels were forgotten. When they got home, Wolverine pulled on the wing to straighten it out. The owl tried to bite him but the attempt was feeble. Wolverine knew the owl was in great pain. Breath fetched some sticks and they tied it all together with caribou sinew. When their doctoring was finished, Wolverine tried to feed the owl, but it was not interested in food. They gave it water and let it sleep, a little puff of white and grey feathers and down, rising and falling with its breathing. They sat there looking at the bird for a long time, looking for any sign of improvement. But healing takes a long time and they had other things to do. They left the bird by their tents and went looking for the mussels.

Wolverine and Breath tended to the owl every day. They named it Ukpigjuaq, Big Owl. They gave it water and sat with it for long periods of time. It seemed a long time before Ukpigjuaq would eat. Wolverine and Breath gave it tender meats from caribou, hare, and whatever small rodents they could catch. They knew owls ate rodents, mostly lemmings and siksiks. They had seen many old droppings of owls and falcons on hilltops. They were always dried-up little furry balls with rodent bones in them. So they trapped lemmings and siksiks to feed the owl. On the beach, they turned rocks over, looking for sculpins. These, too, Ukpigjuaq ate ravenously.

Wolverine also looked after his mother and his little sister as best he could. He fetched water from the river. He put rocks around their tent when the winds picked up and threatened to blow it away. He fished in the river and caught Arctic char, lake trout, and Arctic grayling.

He took his little sister for walks. She was growing fast. Just south of In-there, there are high hills where gyrfalcons nest. When they walked by the cliffs on the sides of those hills, the falcons took flight. When they got close, the falcons swooped down on them, squawking all the while. Wolverine and Little-loved-one would run away, holding their hands over their heads, laughing and laughing. And then, they would go back and do it all over again. When she got tired, Wolverine carried Little-loved-one on his shoulders.

He showed her nests of little birds that he had found in sheltered hollows in the ground. He always told her not to touch the eggs. He said if she did, the little birds might abandon their nests and not come back. He told her they did not like the smell of people. Time went fast. Too soon, the eggs hatched and little furry birds ran along the ground, Wolverine and Little-loved-one right behind them, running after them, catching them, holding them and letting them go again.

Before long, it began to get dark at nights and the winds began to blow more frequently. The tall grasses turned brown and the young birds, the geese, ptarmigans, sandhill cranes, tundra swans, and ducks learned to fly. Thousands of birds had arrived earlier that spring, and now thousands and thousands more would fly south in the fall. The flocks of little birds, snow buntings, phalaropes, sandpipers, and other swift birds taking flight would be the first sign of fall. Wolverine told his little sister about all these things.

Wolverine's father and Paaliaq came back from their dangerous journey with many stories to tell. They had not actually met any people there, but there were signs of life. The Louse-egg-people had been hunting caribou by a large freshwater lake. The-man-with-no-eyebrows and Paaliaq had found caribou carcasses on the shores of a river. They had cut down some trees, taken the wood they needed, and left, feeling like they were stealing from the Louse-egg-people. They said they were happy to be away from there, and walked back as fast as they could, in case they were followed, before they finally stopped to rest.

Wolverine was glad to have his father back. He showed him Ukpigjuaq. He told him about the falcon that had attacked it. He told him about looking after his little sister. He had many stories to tell his father.

"It looks like you did not miss us much. You have been so busy," The-man-with-no-eyebrows said, hugging his son.

Wolverine blushed. "I was beginning to worry you might not come back," he said. "You were away for so long."

The young snowy owl was growing and feeling much better. It ate everything Wolverine and Breath gave it. It hopped around with its wing tied to the sticks, looking like it had a crutch. But it stayed by the tents, usually perched on a rock. It had gotten used to all the people in the small village. Wolverine and Breath had to chase dogs away from it every now and again.

The-man-with-no-eyebrows and Paaliaq set to work building the frames for their kayaks. Their wives took sealskins and soaked them in water for a long time. They scraped all the fur off them and sewed them together to make the skins for the kayaks. Wolverine and Breath watched them work. Wolverine helped bend the ribs into shape, and Breath helped her mother scrape and sew the skins. The two men carefully shaped the wood, drilled holes in the pieces with bow-drills, and tied the frames together with braided caribou sinew. When the frames were completed, the skins were stretched and sewn tightly around them. Paaliaq and The-man-with-no-eyebrows made paddles and launched their kayaks. After trying them out on the lake, they paddled down the river to hunt on the sea.

❖❖❖

One misty morning, Wolverine woke up to find the snowy owl gone. He thought it had flown away, until he remembered it could not bend its right wing because of the splint. He and Breath went out looking for it. A fog had settled over the land and there was dew on the grass. Soon the fish would make their way up the river to lay their eggs in their beds in the lakes. The men would mend the stone fishing weir and repair their fishing spears. With the coming of colder weather, meat would no longer spoil. They would store meat and fish under piles of big rocks to keep it away from the polar bears, the wolverines, and the foxes. It was a time for gathering and preparing food for winter.

They found the owl hopping along the ground, dragging his right wing behind him.

"Are you ready to try out your wings, Ukpigjuaq?" Wolverine said when they had caught up to him.

The owl was now so tame he let them handle him like a pet. They took the splint off and set him on a rock. Ukpigjuaq stood up and folded his wings for the first time, his head held back, turning this way and that, a perfect picture of an owl.

"You look pretty impressive, Ukpigjuaq," Breath said. "Can you fly?"

She picked him up and threw him up into the air. Ukpigjuaq instinctively spread his wings and promptly fell out of the air, rolling over as he hit the ground. "You are not a good lander, Ukpigjuaq," Breath said, laughing.

Wolverine picked him up and again threw him into the air. This time, the owl glided a little longer but his landing was just as rough. "Practise, Ukpigjuaq," Wolverine said. "Practise."

He threw him up in the air again. He and Breath walked home, taking turns picking Ukpigjuaq up and throwing him into the air. In the next few days,

Ukpigjuaq learned to fly, and before winter, he had became a powerful flier like the rest of his kind. Wolverine and Breath no longer fed him, but he always stayed close to them. Wolverine and Breath had a companion for a long time to come.

Beautiful Enough to Take Your Breath Away

It was a few years later. The In-there camp was in full swing. The hunters were away a great deal, hunting caribou for use in the lean times of winter. Caribou bones were buried in big pits by a lake to be made into soup and eaten in winter. They would fish through the ice in the lake and live off the remains of the caribou. Nothing would be wasted.

Down on the beach, some of the men had caught beluga whales. The whales were skinned and butchered. The tender meat along the back was cut into strips and hung up to dry. The sinew was cleaned and dried to be used for thread. The rest of the meat was saved to feed the dogs over the coming winter. The entrails and other pickings were left to the seagulls that always squawk noisily at whale butcherings.

The skin of the whale is called maktaaq. The outer layer is white in full-grown belugas and grey and almost black in young whales. What was not eaten was cached. When the men removed the rocks and collected the maktaaq in winter, much of the fat would have leached into the ground below and the rest of it would be mostly green with age. It was delicious. The same thing would be done with walrus meat and fat.

In late summer, when the sun went down early and the nights were dark, the Arctic char began their yearly climb up the river to spawn. It was then that the men took their pants off and waded into the river up to their waists. Clad only in their coats and their sealskin boots, they set out to repair the saputit, the stone fishing weir. It was a cold job. Fast-flowing water in autumn is always very cold.

A fishing weir has two dams made of rocks, one just above the other. The upriver dam is completely blocked off, so the fish cannot escape through it, except by jumping over the dam. The down-river dam has a rock removed to allow the fish to swim into the space between the two dams. Water flows through the spaces between the rocks but the spaces are too small for the fish to swim through. When there are enough fish between the two dams, a fisherperson wades into the water and puts a rock in the space where the fish were allowed to swim through. Then the fishers wade into the space between the dams and spear the fish with their three-pronged fishing spears. The two outside prongs of the spear are made of curved musk-ox horn. The middle prong is pointed and is made from the leg bone of a caribou.

The-man-with-no-eyebrows and his wife watched their son in the water. He had seen ten-and-four winters now. He was a big boy, taking after his father. It had always been his element: water. Their son was having fun. They watched him standing in the cold water, his spear in his right hand, poised above him. The prongs of the spear touched the water, ready to strike. He watched intently, looking below the surface of the water, waiting for a fish to come within striking distance. He had a flat wooden needle, about the span of his hand long, between his teeth. The needle was attached to a line that trailed downstream in the water. His hand came down and there was splashing in the water as the powerful fish tried to get away from the prongs holding it firmly in place. Wolverine threaded his line through the fish, just behind the gills, in one side, out the other, breaking its spine and killing it instantly. He pulled the prongs of his spear apart and the fish sank back into the water, now attached to the line. Wolverine lifted his arm again, ready to spear another fish.

"Reminds me of you when we first met," Can't-see said with pride in her voice.

"The boy is growing up," The-man-with-no-eyebrows replied.

Filleting fish with her ulu (her woman's knife shaped in a half moon), Breath, too, watched Wolverine fishing with the men. Wolverine was having a wonderful time. He looked up at her and laughed, the leather thong in his mouth, his lips blue with cold. He was a sight to see.

When the weir was empty, the men removed some of the rocks to allow fish a free run up and down the river. They waded ashore and put their pants on. Wolverine was shivering so hard he could hardly talk. He laughed.

"Aaa . . . lia . . . nait," he managed to say to Breath between shivers. "That was fun."

"Ikkii—cold?" Breath asked.

"Ii—yes," Wolverine said.

Upriver, a short distance, Can't-see said to her husband "Our boy is growing. We have to find a wife for him. You should do something about that."

"Yes," The-man-with-no-eyebrows said.

But it was Paaliaq and his wife who supplied the solution to their problem. Over by her tent, Auk, too, was looking at the young couple by the river. "Our daughter looks more beautiful every day," she said to her husband.

"She looks just like you when I came to pick you up many years ago, Wife," Paaliaq said.

"Those two make a nice couple. And they are inseparable. You should talk to The-man-with-no-eyebrows," his wife said.

"Yes," Paaliaq said quietly. And then, he hollered, "The-man-with-no-eyebrows, come and talk with me!"

The-man-with-no-eyebrows walked over to Paaliaq and his wife. When he got there, he looked over at his son and Breath and said, "Your daughter looks beautiful enough to take your breath away."

Paaliaq said, "That is what I wanted to talk to you about." He thought a minute, deciding how to form his words. Finally swallowing his pride, he added, "Many years ago, I was foolish. It takes a man to admit that."

The-man-with-no-eyebrows smiled a wee smile, remembering that night in Paaliaq's igloo, many years before.

Paaliaq glowered at him. "If you tell me I was short-tempered, I will knock you across the river," he said.

The-man-with-no-eyebrows put on his best serious face. "No." He told a small lie. "I was thinking no such thought."

Out of the corner of his eye, he could just see that Auk had a faint smile in the corner of her mouth. She, too, was remembering that night.

Paaliaq asked, "Have you made other arrangements for your son's marriage?"

The-man-with-no-eyebrows said, "No. We have made no arrangements. Not knowing what is to happen to my son when he is of age to marry, we have not sought a wife for him these past years."

"I never should have refused the request you made so honourably," Paaliaq said, formally. "Now, since you have not made any other arrangements for your son's marriage, I would like to return the request you made long ago. When your son is of age to marry, may we offer our daughter?"

This was completely unexpected, and caught The-man-with-no-eyebrows by surprise. A heavy lump came into his throat and tears welled in his eyes. It was so sudden. He was suddenly filled with a great happiness. The fear of what might happen to his son was lifted from his chest. He swallowed the lump in his throat and managed to say, "Your offer is accepted with the greatest of pleasure. I will do my best to teach my unworthy son to provide for your daughter."

"And I will attempt to teach my daughter well," Auk said.

"I thank you," The-man-with-no-eyebrows said to Auk.

Turning back to Paaliaq, The-man-with-no-eyebrows began to say, "There is that little matter of never setting foot on this land . . ."

But Paaliaq interrupted him one more time. "Do not worry about that little matter," he said. "What was said in anger is forgotten. There will be no curse on my son-in-law-to-be."

"You have filled my heart with a great happiness, Paaliaq," The-man-with-no-eyebrows said, and turning to Auk, added with a slight bow, "And, you too, Auk. Now I would like to deliver this good news to my wife."

The-man-with-no-eyebrows returned to his wife to give her the news.

"What did Paaliaq want?" Can't-see asked.

The-man-with-no-eyebrows replied, "He asked if we would consent to Wolverine marrying his daughter."

"What wonderful news," Can't-see said.

Little-loved-one's ears perked up. "Uh, huh!" she yelled. "Big Brother's going to have a wife. Big Brother's going to have a baby. Big Brother and Breath. Naananaanaa!"

She danced around their tent, singing about what Big Brother was going to do, getting louder and louder.

Wolverine blushed. He grabbed Little-loved-one and wrestled her to the ground. "Not right away!" he said when he had her firmly locked in his arms.

Little-loved-one only laughed and yelled, struggling to get away, "Big Brother and Breath are going away together."

She was incorrigible. There was joy and happiness in their small family. Things would work out all right.

It was shortly after that that the camp broke up and people moved away. The tents were taken down and the gear was packed up. The few dogs people had brought with them were loaded with packs full of dried provisions, bedding, and other odds and ends. The people carried what they could for the long trek back to their fall and winter hunting grounds. The-man-with-no-eyebrows and his family would trek back up north to where Wolverine was born. They would hunt seals, whales, walruses, and polar bears on the sea ice. Paaliaq and his family would go south for a time and look for more caribou, and then, they would return to the sea. Somewhere in their travels, they would meet again, most likely at Bit-of-sand just before spring came. They said their good-byes and went their separate ways.

And so, everything was restored to the way it should have been. Wolverine would have a wife when he became of age. And the curse, so hastily brought upon him, was revoked. Or, so they thought. . . .

A Most Disagreeable Creature

As The-man-with-no-eyebrows and his family left, a pair
of beady eyes watched from under a big slab of rock.
Hatred showed in those beady eyes and it was obvious
they meant to do mischief. Old Mr. Siksik hated everyone. He crawled out from under the rock and glared
at the departing family. He stared after them until they
were out of sight.

Old Mr. Siksik glared at most everyone these days.
He had lived a long time, a very long time for a siksik.
And he still had a long, miserable life left to live.

There was a time when Old Mr. Siksik was young
and played with other young siksiks. They ran, played
tag, and rolled on the ground with complete abandon,
as young siksiks will. He had a sister he romped with
before that first winter. His mother gathered food for

them, stuffing her cheeks with succulent plants, and stored them in the burrow they would live in through the cold winter. He and his sister helped, of course, but it was his mother who did the real work. He and his sister had time to play. Those were nice times spent running and exploring in the long, bright months of summer. At the first sign of impending danger, his mother would whistle, loud and shrill, and he and his sister would scramble into their hole in the ground and laugh, *"Chh, chh, chhh, chhh!!!"* when they were safely inside.

But he did not think about those times now. With the coming of the first cold season, a strong shaman had needed a tuurnngaq and he, Mr. Siksik, had been chosen. He was proud to have been chosen. It was a very respectable appointment. To become a magic animal for a powerful shaman meant great honour. But that was long ago.

In his first winter as a tuurnngaq, a dark cloud had settled over his mind and it had stayed there. Now he was old. It had not been a happy life for Old Mr. Siksik. He had worked hard for his master. Now, he was tired and he hated his master. He hated everyone. It was not easy being a magic animal attached to Paaliaq. The magic part was easy; he could do it in his sleep. The mean curses Paaliaq uttered when he was being short-tempered were the easiest. He loved those. It was the good that Paaliaq did that irked him and made him furious. If only he could do magic without being bidden to do it, he would create such havoc the world of the shaman would be destroyed forever. But he could not do magic without a command from his master. And whatever his shaman commanded of him, he was bound to do. That was annoying. However, he had figured out a way to get around that little problem somewhat. He was clever when he wanted to be devious. But he was still a siksik and a siksik leads a hard life.

Paaliaq was a wanderer, a nomad. Old Mr. Siksik followed him in his travels wherever he went. He had followed him for many winters now. And a siksik is not really equipped to travel long distances. He has short legs and delicate feet with long slender fingers. But Paaliaq travelled everywhere, helping people. He travelled up and down the west coast of Hudson Bay and inland, as far as the trees. And Old Mr. Siksik had to follow him.

Paaliaq spent his winters out on the cold, windy sea ice, hunting seals. He showed absolutely no regard for his faithful tuurnngaq; shamans make no direct contact with their magic animals. Paaliaq was always aware of the presence of his tuurnngaq, but he had never once touched him; he had never even looked at him. That was the way of the shamans.

It was freezing out there on the sea ice. Old Mr. Siksik had more than once risked his life by cuddling up to Paaliaq's mean dogs for warmth, only to be barked at and snapped at with sharp teeth, and sent scurrying to spend the night, shivering, under ice and snow.

And there were the Arctic white foxes. They followed hunters everywhere. They were always looking for scraps the hunters might leave behind. And they were always after him. Old Mr. Siksik had a scar on his cheek. A fox had once dug through the snow and ice, trying to get at him. When that fox got too close, Old Mr. Siksik had bit it hard on its lip and hung on, swinging from side to side as the fox tried to throw him off. He had tasted the blood of that fox. The fox had scratched his cheek with its claws, trying to get rid of him. But old Mr. Siksik had hung on until the fox had had enough. It had gone off running and yelping because of the pain. Old Mr. Siksik thought of that little fight with a gleam in his eye and rubbed his scar with his long, slender fingers. It was one of the few thoughts he relished. The experience had been worth the scar.

But other thoughts were not so pleasant. Like the time Paaliaq just had to paddle his kayak out to an island and spend some time meditating or something, contemplating some good he wanted to do. It was not far, but Old Mr. Siksik had swum hard, his little fingers barely moving him along. He had climbed onto the rocky beach and shivered like he was never going to stop, letting the sun dry the water off his fur. Did Paaliaq not know that siksiks were not meant to swim?

No, siksiks have never been swimmers. Their paws are not built for swimming; they are thin and hand-like, with no skin between the fingers with which to paddle. Siksiks are afraid of water. When they are wet, they don't even have enough sense to shake the water off their fur like dogs do. No wonder Old Mr. Siksik hated swimming to the island.

Then Paaliaq had turned right around and paddled his kayak straight back to the mainland. And Old Mr. Siksik had to follow him back, swimming with all his might. He had not even warmed up enough to stop shivering. It was night and it was cold when he finally made it back to shore. He had shivered all night, waiting for the sun to return, thinking he would surely die. Not only was he cold, he had nearly drowned in the waves on the trip back.

And then, there were the old women. Oh, how he hated the old women. They had all the respect of everyone. They cooked. They prepared food for winter. They dispensed wisdom, their eyes having seen many years of mistakes and good works, their ears having heard wise words and folly, and their hearts having known grief and joy. But they hated siksiks. Even Paaliaq's wrinkly old mother hated siksiks. Whenever old women saw a siksik, they would yell and scream and climb on the highest rock to get away from it. Everyone would go after the siksik, throwing stones, just to please the silly old things. Sometimes Old Mr. Siksik walked up to old women just to get them screaming. Then he would hide in the deepest burrow and snigger, *"Chuckle, chuckle, chuckle . . ."* until people forgot about him.

Most of all, Old Mr. Siksik hated boys. Boys were always practising to become masters in the art of hunting. And they practised on siksiks. They threw stones. They rocked big slabs of stone the poor siksiks were hiding under, back and forth, back and forth, trying to force them out, so they could stone them. They tried to smoke them out. And they tried to make them come out by pouring water into their holes and drowning them. Old Mr. Siksik had, many a time, shouted at the mean boys, *"Ch, ch, ch, ch!!!"* shaking with fear, hiding under a rock.

He had been hit by well-thrown rocks. His flimsy fingers had been broken more than once by boys practising their hunting skills. Yes, Old Mr. Siksik hated boys most of all. And Wolverine was a boy. He hated Wolverine.

The other day, when Paaliaq had said, "Do not worry about that little matter. What was said in anger is forgotten. There will be no curse on my Son-in-law-to-be," Old Mr. Siksik had decided that he was old and very hard of hearing. He had covered his ears and mumbled, *"Mumble, mumble, mumble . . ."* trying not to hear Paaliaq. This way, he did not have to remove the curse as he was bidden; he had not heard it. Now, all he had to do was to wait for the right moment, and Wolverine would never set foot "on this land" again. He knew what that meant and he anticipated it with relish. This thought pleased him very much.

The next day, Paaliaq and his family crossed the river and headed south. The rains of autumn had swelled the inland lakes and the rivers flowed strong. Old Mr. Siksik, crossing the river at the stone weir, lost his footing, and was carried downstream a long way. He was swept over a rapids, and was almost at sea when he finally made it to the other shore. He was shivering with the cold, damp winds of autumn and nearly drowned, when he finally dragged his old body onto the rocks. He shivered so hard, he thought he would never stop. And his teeth chattered so loudly he thought they would shatter to bits. Oh, he hated Paaliaq. He wished Paaliaq would lose his temper completely and curse himself to the moon. But then, he would have to follow him there and he did not know how he would do that.

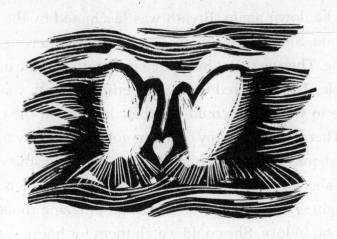

Not Just a Pretty Girl

Just south of In-there is a lake called Naujatujuq—Many-seagulls. No one really knows why this lake is called Many-seagulls because there are hardly ever any seagulls there. But there are fish in Many-seagulls, lots of fish: lake trout and land-locked char, mostly. Paaliaq and his family stopped there for a time. They stayed until the lakes froze over and snow came. When the ice on Many-seagulls was thick enough to carry their weight, they chiselled holes in it and fished.

When the lakes freeze over and the snow falls in large, lazy flakes, the caribou get lazy. They walk around slowly, like they have all the time in the world to do absolutely nothing. Huge bulls with giant antlers lie in the soft snow, watching over the other caribou. They get up and follow the others around for a while, and then they lie down again. Breath was fascinated by the fall caribou. She watched them. They were not interested in eating. They were not interested in Breath and the other people. They ignored them. Sometimes Breath was so close to them, she could see their breaths in the cool air. There were so many of them, not in any hurry to go anywhere. One day, while she was watching the caribou, she wondered why they were so lazy. And then she thought, *They are in love!* It was an amazing thought: caribou in love. She could watch them for hours.

But this year, her mother would not let her. Her mother seemed to have decided on something. She was insistent. She was in a hurry. She had always hurried about at this time of the year. Sealskins needed to be scraped. Caribou skins needed to be dried. There was much cutting and sewing to do. But while she worked, she had always let Breath explore and discover the wonders of the world about her on her own. Now, for some reason, Breath was no longer allowed to be idle. This time, her mother needed her help in everything she did. Carefully, Breath scraped the inner membrane off a wet sealskin with her ulu, her mother forever insisting, "Carefully, carefully! Do not cut the skin."

Breath and her mother scraped off the inner membrane, called mamiq, with their ulus. They washed the oil off the skin, scraped the fur off, dried the skin (a most wonderful product known as qisik—tough, warm, and durable), tanned it, and made it into boots called kamiik, the waterproof, knee-high workboots Inuit wore on most occasions. Breath was suddenly the scraper, the drier, and the tanner of skins.

Carefully, she cut a piece of ugjuk skin into an oval shape, just larger than a foot. She tanned it, forever chewing on it, kneading it, and chewing again, until it was soft and pliable. Carefully, with her mother's words in her ear, "Tenderly. Don't cut too much off," she shaved the edges until they were thin and even all around.

Breath worked at the kamiik, making the leggings and carefully sewing the soles on. She had to redo the soles many times; they kept twisting. When she was finally finished them, she gave them to her father.

"For me?" her father said.

"Yes, father," Breath said.

He put them on. He did a little dance, looking at his feet. He laughed a good-natured laugh.

"A little twisted but they will improve," he said. "My girl is learning."

He hugged her. Breath blushed, but she was happy. Paaliaq wore those kamiik throughout the winter.

Over the winter, her mother spent most days teaching her how to work with caribou hides—amiq. Caribou drop their fur in spring. They grow new fur in the fall. This new fur is the material they used to make the rest of their clothing. Auk taught her daughter how to cut the hides for clothing: the sleeves had to be cut in such a way that the underarms did not bunch up and feel uncomfortable for the wearer, the chest had to have thinner fur so as not to restrict movement, the nap of the fur had to flow properly to prevent rubbing. There was so much to learn.

Paaliaq finally wore out his kamiik in spring. Even then, he would not give them up. He kept them, folded neatly, like a memento, celebrating a great and passing event. By then, Breath had made him a whole new suit of clothes, a caribou-skin inner coat, a thick outer coat, mitts, soft and supple caribou-skin pants, thick outer boots with bearskin bottoms, and every other piece of clothing a man needed to live in their harsh climate. Sometimes the clothes did not fit properly. They bunched up here and there. Sometimes the stitching was uneven, but Paaliaq never complained. He wore his clothes proudly. The clothes ripped and wore thin with everyday wear and tear. Breath mended them with increasing efficiency. She was a willing student and she learned her job well.

Before she knew it, the days were longer and the caribou were coming back. They were no longer in love. They seemed to have a purpose. They were on the move in huge numbers, thousands and thousands of them, mostly females and young males, relentlessly heading north.

"Where are they all going?" Breath asked.

"They are going north and inland," her mother said. "They are going to the place where they have their calves."

"They have a special place to do that?" Breath asked.

Her mother replied, "Yes. Like us, they like to go to a safe place to have their babies. They go back to that same place every year, a place where they can keep an eye on the wolves that are always after their babies."

"Oh," Breath said.

She had always thought animals just lived wherever they were, just ate and moved on with no rhyme or reason. But now, she was beginning to understand they thought and planned and reasoned like everyone else. They cared for their young like everyone else. She learned that the world had an order to it.

As if sensing this new-found knowledge in his daughter, Paaliaq, too, one day decided to head north. They packed up their belongings and trekked north to In-there. It was a long journey. From Many-seagulls, they had made their way south, travelling on the sea ice, finally coming ashore as the ice floated out to sea. Now it was time to start the cycle all over again.

As they made their way north, Paaliaq said to his daughter, "I think it may be time you practised making clothing for someone else."

"Who?" Breath asked.

"You have too many questions," Paaliaq said, laughing.

But he did not answer her question.

Marble Island

Early one morning, The-man-with-no-eyebrows climbed the hill behind his tent. He sat there for some time, looking up at the sky and out toward the horizon. There were a few light, wispy clouds to the south, high up in the sky. Otherwise, the sky was a cool, clear blue. The wind was calm. It would be a good day.

The-man-with-no-eyebrows looked to the east. Way out on the sea, he saw Marble Island floating just above the horizon. It had been a long time since he had been there. He remembered exploring the island with his father. It seemed so many years ago but he remembered it well: the white, smooth outcrops, the white rocks on brown, mossy ground, the whales, the seals, and the great bowhead whales that blew puffs of steam way up into the air. He remembered the Arctic hare that disappeared as soon as they stopped moving because they were as white as the rocks beside them. It was time he went there again. It was time he took his son there.

The-man-with-no-eyebrows went home, woke Wolverine and said, "Son, gather your things. We are going out to Uqsuriak to see if there are whales about."

"Yes, Father," Wolverine said. Excitement welled in his chest.

He and his father had taken the long walk to the land of the trees, that summer. He had built his own kayak, and after a month of paddling around the islands close to In-there, he had become quite a good paddler.

Little-loved-one said, "Can I come, too?"

"No," her father said. "We are going by kayak and we have no room for you. It is a long way. Sometimes, it gets very rough and you might fall off if I took you."

There was room for only one person in a kayak. The-man-with-no-eyebrows could, of course, transport Little-loved-one lying prone on the rear deck of his kayak, but it was dangerous and he would only do it if he needed to go a short distance.

Little-loved-one stamped her feet on the ground. "I never get to go anywhere," she said and stomped off.

As if in a dream, Wolverine set about sharpening his sakku—his harpoon head—fumbling with the sharpening stone, his mind already on Marble Island. Carefully, he placed his harpoon and his killing spear in their places on the foredeck of his kayak. He inflated his seal float and tied it to his harpoon line and secured it behind his seat. His mother gave him provisions and a container of fresh water. Putting his waterproof sealskin clothing on, he was ready.

On a rock nearby, Ukpigjuaq sat. "We are going to Marble Island," Wolverine said. "Are you coming?"

Ukpigjuaq lazily blinked his yellow eyes, swivelled his head on his shoulders, and gracefully flew off, heading out to sea. That bird was amazing. He seemed to understand what Wolverine said to him.

Wolverine was excited. Marble Island had always been a mystery to him. Sometimes when he was on a high hill, he could see the island, suspended in the air just above the horizon, like a mirage. It was all white. He had seen it up close when he and his father had hunted seals on the floe edge, out there, where the solid ice ends and the ice floes move constantly with the tides and currents. But he had never actually been there. As far as he knew, the sea had never frozen all the way to the island in his lifetime. Between where he was and the island, there was always water and moving ice in winter.

He wondered if it had, at one time, been a giant ice floe as legend told. He had heard the story of how an old woman had been set adrift on an ice floe and how that ice floe had been transformed into Marble Island to give the old woman a solid footing. He thought, *How else could a whole island in the middle of the ocean be all white?* Sometimes, man could be so mean to his fellow man, but as the first Kiviuq story taught, nature always provided for the poor, unwanted people. Perhaps the story was true.

Wolverine and his father paddled east, out past Big-igloo Island and Soapstone Island, and then they struck out over open sea to the white island. Seals popped their heads up out of the water, but Wolverine and his father paid them no mind. There were flocks of ducks and guillemots flying low over the calm water, diving and feeding on the little fish below. As Wolverine silently dipped his paddle, side to side into the gentle swells, his anticipation grew. It was a whole new experience for him. Wolverine and his father were practised paddlers, but it took them all day to reach Marble Island.

The island is seventeen kilometres long, lying east to west, and four kilometres wide. On the east end is a channel where one can drive a boat through at high tide. At its west end is a small round harbour with a narrow entrance on the south side. The island is white. It is made of tunnuujaq, caribou-fat rock, or quartzite. It looks not unlike marble. In late afternoon, The-man-with-no-eyebrows and his son rounded the southwest end of the island and landed.

The-man-with-no-eyebrows said, "You have to crawl up the beach a short distance."

"Why?" Wolverine asked.

"Lest death should befall you before summer comes again," his father said.

Wolverine crawled. He and his father carried their kayaks up the beach, ate, and were soon asleep in a sheltered place. It had been a long day and they slept soundly. In the morning, they again shoved off, and spent the day chasing whales and seals around the island. The whales were wary and they could not get close enough for a harpoon strike. Paddling along the south shore of the island, they caught a couple of seals. They towed them to the island, skinned them, packed, and headed home. They had just rounded the southwest point of the island and were on a homeward tack, when a wind picked up. It rose to such intensity that they had to return to wait for fairer weather. As soon as they landed, the wind stopped and the sea became still again. This was very unusual.

They shoved off again and headed home, and again, the wind rose. They tried to keep going, but the wind got stronger and stronger and they had to return to the island again. And again, as soon as they landed, the wind stopped and the sea became still.

The-man-with-no-eyebrows said, "This is most unusual. You rest awhile, Son. I am going out to see what is going on."

The-man-with-no-eyebrows paddled his kayak toward the mainland. Nothing happened. The sea remained calm.

After a short while, he was out of sight and Wolverine was alone on Marble Island. Wolverine looked about him, wondering what he should do; he was all alone on this bare, white, silent island.

Wolverine got into his kayak and started to follow his father, but again, the wind picked up and he had to abandon his attempt. The waters calmed as soon as he landed. He tried again, and again was driven back by heavy winds. It seemed the sea was playing tricks on him. Every time he tried to go to the mainland, the wind picked up and he was driven back to the island. He unloaded his kayak and paddled around the island. Nothing happened. He headed for the mainland and the wind and heavy seas returned. Puzzled, he set up camp, built a fire, and waited for his father.

Not long afterward, Ukpigjuaq came and perched on a rock. He settled for a long wait. Wolverine looked up and said, "Looks like it's just you and me, Ukpigjuaq."

Ukpigjuaq swivelled his head around, looked squarely at Wolverine, and blinked. They waited all afternoon, and eventually, the sun circled the sky, slowly sank, touched the horizon to the northwest, and disappeared. They waited in twilight, and eventually, the sun reappeared above the horizon again. Wolverine and Ukpigjuaq waited all day. It was afternoon when The-man-with-no-eyebrows returned.

"I have been paddling out," Wolverine said when his father had landed. "It is most puzzling. When I paddle around the island, nothing happens, but as soon as I head for home, the wind picks up. If I keep going, the wind just gets higher and higher until I have to come back."

They were in the small sheltered bay at the west end of Marble Island. The-man-with-no-eyebrows looked about him.

"I have to go back," he said. "You need shelter. There is a cave, well actually, a hole in the ground just to the east of here, against the south shore, over there."

He pointed east over a white hill.

"But Father, what is happening? Why are you leaving me here?" Wolverine said. He was beginning to feel like an unwanted boy, helpless.

"You cannot seem to get off this island, Son," he said. "I must go and find Paaliaq. He has to know something about these strange goings-on. I have to try to find out what is happening."

"Father, am I going to be stuck here forever?" Wolverine asked in a panic.

"There has to be an explanation. I have to find Paaliaq and ask him about it," The-man-with-no-eyebrows said. "I will bring you more provisions when I return. In the meantime, you have enough food. Go to the cave and set up camp. The cave opens out to the sea on the south side and to a small, freshwater pond to the north. You can take shelter there. But you must leave a present for it when you leave. Now, I have to go before nightfall. Fare well, Son. Here-you-are."

"There-you-go, Father," Wolverine returned the good-bye gesture. "Hurry back," he added with a sinking heart.

Cursed

The-man-with-no-eyebrows looked back at his son as
he paddled away from the island. Wolverine seemed so
small and vulnerable, his little boy. Whoever had caused
this thing was a very mean person. It made The-man-
with-no-eyebrows mad. But he gathered up his cour-
age, tried not to show his anger and the fear that made
his heart sink. His son stood there, looking so small, all
alone. The-man-with-no-eyebrows swallowed the lump
in this throat and forced the tears from wetting his eyes.
He paddled away.

He had to find out why his son was stuck on this
wretched island. Somebody had caused this strange
thing to happen. He would find out who. He would do
something to that person. He did not know what, but
the person had better watch out. The-man-with-no-eye-

brows was very mad. He did not get mad often, but Wolverine was his little boy and nobody messed with his family.

The-man-with-no-eyebrows returned to the mainland and sought Paaliaq out. He found him and his family at Bit-of-sand. They were trekking north to prepare for winter at Big Rapids. After greeting Paaliaq, The-man-with-no-eyebrows asked him for his help. "My son cannot seem to get off Uqsuriak," he said. "Every time he tries to paddle away from the island, a big wind comes and the sea begins to boil. What has he done to deserve this?"

Paaliaq thought for a while. Presently, he said, "I have to saka. I have to go into a shamanic trance and conjure up my tuurnngaq. I have to ask him why my son-in-law-to-be cannot get off the island."

He began to walk in a circle. He put his left hand over his eyes, and swinging his right hand by his side, he began his slow dance. And as he danced, he chanted, "Pamiuq, pamiuq, pamiuq—tail, tail, tail . . ."

He did this for a long time. The-man-with-no-eyebrows and Paaliaq's family watched. At one point, Paaliaq increased his tempo and yelled out his mantra, "PAMIUQ, PAMIUQ!!!"

Eventually, he settled back into a slow, trance-like state, his left hand still cupped over his face, his right hand swinging slowly. Finally, he stopped, exhausted.

When he lowered his left hand, concern and fear showed on his face. Slowly, he raised his head and said, "How could I do this to my son-in-law-to-be? I have cursed him to the island, and now, I cannot bring him back."

"What do you mean by that?" The-man-with-no-eyebrows asked, anger beginning to rise in his chest.

Paaliaq explained. "Do you remember when you first came to ask me for my daughter?"

"Yes," The-man-with-no-eyebrows said.

Paaliaq continued, "I was mad and I said 'When your son is of age to marry, he will never set foot on this land again.' That was the curse. Well, he is not on this land anymore; he is down there on that island. And he cannot return to the mainland. That was the curse and it is working."

"Why did Father curse Wolverine?" Breath asked her mother.

"Because you were crying," her mother answered.

"What?" Breath said in disbelief.

Frustrated, her mother said, "Never mind. I will explain later."

The-man-with-no-eyebrows yelled at Paaliaq, "But you removed the curse! You told me so yourself!!"

"Well," Paaliaq said, "my tuurngaq is either deaf or he is not listening to me. I cannot seem to get him to remove the curse."

The-man-with-no-eyebrows' anger welled up inside his body. *This is the man who cursed my son,* he thought. *He cursed my little boy.* Without thinking, he balled up his huge hands into fists and flexed his muscles in his chest. And then his right hand moved, it seemed, of its own accord. It moved so fast, no one saw it, until his fist had landed on the side of Paaliaq's head. Paaliaq went flying through the air and landed on his back on the ground.

The-man-with-no-eyebrows stepped forward, anger in his face, but Auk grabbed his arm and yelled, "No!"

The-man-with-no-eyebrows looked at Auk. She was holding his arm, trembling with fear. He said, "I'm sorry. I didn't mean to do that," and gently removed her hand from his arm.

He looked at Paaliaq and yelled, "What are you going to do now? My son is stuck on Uqsuriak because of you! You got him stuck on that island; you get him back!"

Paaliaq's left temple began to swell and turn blue. He did not move to counter The-man-with-no-eyebrows' attack. It seemed a little voice in his head told him, *Stay calm,* and for once in his life, he listened to it. Here was an angry man who had every right to be angry with him. To fight back would only provoke him. And Paaliaq understood The-man-with-no-eyebrows' anger. He would be angry, too, if someone had cursed his family.

He stood back up. Calmly, he said, "The-man-with-no-eyebrows, I will try to get through to my tuurnngaq.

I will get him to hear my command one way or another. I will remove the curse."

To Auk, he said, "Wife, you continue on the journey. Take what you can. I will catch up with you. I am going back to In-there where I recruited that wretched animal. I want to go and saka on his old siksik mound and see if I can get through to him."

To The-man-with-no-eyebrows, he said, "I will get your son back if I have to wring my tuurnngaq's neck to do it." And then, touching the bruise on his face, he added with a tentative smile, "You hit really hard. It is a good thing you are on my side."

He walked off, westward.

On a hillside, a pair of beady eyes watched Paaliaq from under a rock. If Old Mr. Siksik could smile, his face would have been one big, contented smirk. He was not going to follow Paaliaq to In-there today. Maybe he would follow him tomorrow; maybe he would not. He was old and tired and hard of hearing. And it was a beautiful day. He would sleep in the sun and rest a while.

Missing Wolverine

After her father left, Breath said, "What did you mean by Father cursing Wolverine because I was crying?"

Her mother said, "When The-man-with-no-eyebrows came to ask for you, you were crying. That made your father angry. He said "No" to The-man-with-no-eyebrows and cursed Wolverine."

"But why?" Breath protested. "I was only a baby. Babies cry."

Her mother said "Well, sometimes your father's temper gets the best of him."

Breath understood. Her father was like that. She turned away. She needed to be by herself. She walked along the beach and looked at the white island floating above the horizon. Wolverine was down there, all by himself. She missed him. She had never learned to paddle a kayak and there was no other way to get to the island. It was a dangerous crossing. She could not go down there.

How could my father do this to you? she thought. *And just because I was crying? I was a baby. Babies cry. People don't get stuck on islands just because babies cry.* This boy she had spent so much time with was now stuck on an island. She could no longer see him. She missed him like she had never missed anyone before. "Will I ever see you again?" she asked in the direction of the island.

And she felt something else she had never felt before, a stirring in her breast; a longing. She longed to lie in the sun with Wolverine and just look at the roof of the big sky above them. She longed to lie there with him for a long time. And . . . maybe . . . to turn over and look at his smiling face, and maybe . . . to touch that wispy bit of a beard that was beginning to grow on his chin. She could see him so clearly in her mind, as if he was right there with her.

It was a funny thought, this thought of touching him. She had never thought to touch him before. It was a strange kind of feeling, but she kind of liked it. And maybe he would touch her. She shivered at the thought. And then she realized she wanted to hug him more than anything in the whole world. She wanted to hug him and cry, to wet his face with her tears, and to laugh.

She wanted to hug him for the rest of her life. Walking along the beach, she thought about him for a long time. And she realized she was crying. She stopped and sat on a big rock. Big salty tears rolled down her cheeks. She missed that boy on that island. She sat there on that beach and cried for a long time. Her cries came in big sobs that shook her whole body. When she finally stopped crying, she returned to her mother to prepare for the trip to Big Rapids.

When all the packing was done, they left. As she walked, Breath kept looking back. Her mother noticed her looking back toward the sea and the island. She saw her looking back long after they could no longer see the island or the sea. But she said nothing. Her daughter was growing up. She was glad about that, but she was also sad about Wolverine being all alone on Uqsuriak. What if her husband could not remove the curse? What if Wolverine could never return again? What if her daughter had to grow up never having a husband, never having children . . . to grow old, and be all alone? She knew her daughter was devoted to Wolverine. Even if The-man-with-no-eyebrows and his family released her from her commitment, she would never take another husband. Auk tried not to think of what might happen. Then she noticed she was crying.

◆◆◆

The-man-with-no-eyebrows felt a little better after hitting Paaliaq. His temper cooled and he thought about what he should do. His first thought was to provide for his son. He went home, took some bedding and provisions, and headed back to the island. He kept thinking about that helpless little boy, all alone on a lonely, desolate island in the middle of the huge bay. How did these things happen? In anger, mere mortals did and said things they did not intend. Others heard those words and took them to heart. Sometimes, there was no turning back. That is the way things happened.

The Great Practice

Back on the island, Wolverine had watched his father paddle away. Then he had said, "Let's go find a home, Ukpigjuaq."

Wolverine and Ukpigjuaq found a giant hole in the white rock at the south side of the island. From above, it looked like some huge person had dug a hole in the ground to make a pond for his pet whale. At the bottom of this hole was a clear, turquoise-coloured pond, big enough to paddle his kayak in. Wolverine climbed down the rocky sides of the hole and walked along the shore of the pond, clinging to the sides of the hole. On the south side of this hole was a cave, the size of a good-sized igloo. It had two entrances. The northern entrance opened to the turquoise pond. The southern entrance opened to a sort of balcony on the sheer cliff wall of the island with pounding surf down below. It was not comfortable, but it would do for the time being. Wolverine climbed back up to fetch his gear. As it turned out, he was marooned a bit longer than he thought he would be.

When The-man-with-no-eyebrows returned, he explained to his son what had happened.

"My Son," he said, "long ago, you were cursed never to set foot on the mainland when you became of age to marry. That time is now. The curse, uttered in a time of unwarranted anger and without good reason, seems to have taken effect. Paaliaq is working to remove it. Until he does, I am afraid you have to stay here."

"Yes, Father," Wolverine said simply. His heart sank.

As soon as his father said he had been cursed, Wolverine knew who had cursed him. There was only one person he knew who had the ability to cast a spell. But he could not say anything against that person because that person was his father-in-law-to-be. He could not think anything bad of him. The most revered people in the world were one's in-laws, revered even more than one's own parents or elders. They were treated with the utmost respect. To think badly of them was an unforgivable sin. He could not call them by name for fear of insulting them; he could barely allow himself to look at them. He would stand by them and show them every respect until his dying day. That was the way of his people. There was nothing to say.

The-man-with-no-eyebrows said, "I have to return to your mother and sister for a time. I will be back."

And there Wolverine was, all alone. He sat by himself and cried. He cried for a long time, like he had not cried since he was a little boy. He could not hold the tears back. They just came and ran down his face in huge drops. He was alone. There was no one else. Would he have to spend the rest of his life here? Alone? He had never felt so alone in his life.

When he finally stopped crying, Wolverine wandered around Marble Island. He explored the caves, the rocky landscape, the seashell-strewn beaches, and the sheltered harbours. There was much to see. From a hilltop at the east end of the island, he could see all around. To the west, way off in the distance, he could see an island sticking straight up: Soapstone Island. Beyond that were Big-igloo Island and the mainland. To the north was the closest point of land: Bit-of-sand. To the south and east, there was water, the great Salt, as far as the eye could see.

Marble Island is an incredibly amazing place. It is rocky and hilly. On a sunny day, the fine sand in the dried-up puddles up in the hills is so pure white, it is blinding. In summer the ground is covered with tiny flowers and berries. Butterflies and moths flutter around and light on the white rocks and tundra plants. In some places, the rock outcropping shows notches in a regular pattern. They look like they have been gouged by a huge file. The sand looks like filings from that giant file. There are two caves, one on the south side, one on the north. In the sea around it, seals and ducks abound. On some days, one can see the giant bowhead whales blowing air out through the tops of their heads in the deep water to the east; they create a mist that flies way up in the air. White beluga whales and their grey young cling to the shores, hiding from killer whales. And polar bears are regular visitors.

Out at sea, when the tide ebbs and the water level goes down, you can see a lot farther away. When the tide rises again, what you see may disappear over the horizon.

Wolverine sat on a white rock on the hilltop and watched the animals: the seals, the walruses, whales, and polar bears. He paddled around in his kayak, testing the way home now and again and finding, always, that the sea still played tricks on him. Ukpigjuaq stayed with him, his only constant companion, flying above him as he paddled his kayak.

His father came to bring him new clothes, more food, more flints to start fires, news from home, and whatever he needed to sustain him until the business of the curse was resolved.

Wolverine blocked the entrance to his cave that opened out to sea with skins his father brought him. At the east end of the island, the rocks peeled apart in huge sheets. Wolverine carried some of these sheets to his cave and fashioned a low table. He gathered lichen and moss, cleaned them up, and made himself a bed. His blankets were caribou skins his father brought him. He carried water from the freshwater pond just outside his doorway. He was comfortable.

When the berries were ripe, he picked them and saved them. He cached meat and maktaaq as he had always done, preparing for the winter months when game would be scarce. He made himself needles out of caribou leg bone. He dried whale sinew to use for thread. He fashioned a qulliq, a seal-oil lamp, out of stone. He dried lichen to use for kindling. In the low-lying areas where the ground was wet, he found cotton grass. He picked the cotton and, mixing it with dried moss, he made wicking for his qulliq. After these labours, he was ready for a long stay.

Wolverine was getting pretty independent, and as he worked, he took pride in his independence. Every morning he made himself a broth with seal meat and roots. The rich seal oil in this broth kept him warm throughout the day. It fuelled his body. Sometimes he ate dried caribou jerky, mikku, that his father had brought. He fished in the little bay between the island and an adjoining island that would one day be known as Dead Man Island.

When the work was done, his mind wandered.

He missed his mother and his little sister. In these long hours, Wolverine would sit on a hilltop looking at the mainland. It looked so close but it was also so far away. If only he could fly across . . . But he also knew the way was not the problem. The problem was that he could not set foot on the land across the way. Even if he could manage to get across that stretch of ocean, he could not set foot on that land. Something would happen to prevent him from doing so. As fall came, and turned to winter, he did not dwell on the problem of getting across; he thought of Breath more and more.

Breath was there somewhere in that land across the way. He saw her walking, with her springy gait, the way she turned, her coat with the big hood, and her long black hair swinging with her when she turned. Sometimes he saw her as if she was there in front of him. He wanted to walk with her. He wanted to see her smile. He remembered her laughing after he and the men had fished at the stone weir. He was so cold his lips were swollen and his mouth did not work properly. And he had shivered. He had shivered so hard he could barely talk. Funny he should remember her laugh. It was the true happiness and pleasure in her eyes he remembered. Oh, to hear her laugh again. . . .

And he remembered her fingers. They were long and slender. He wanted to hold them in his hands. He wanted to look into her eyes. He wanted to see her smile. Her eyelashes were so black she looked like she had shadows on her eyelids. He remembered how beautiful her eyes were. They were a deep brown colour and they twinkled when she smiled. He felt a flutter in his chest. It was love that made his heart flutter, a love for someone he might never see again. His breast swelled and he cried again.

On a rock, Ukpigjuaq swivelled his head and looked to the mainland. Then he swivelled his head again. He looked straight at Wolverine and blinked. *He knows*, Wolverine thought. "Go and tell Breath I miss her," he said.

Ukpigjuaq swivelled his head once again, spread his wings, flapped once, and flew up into the air. He headed for the mainland. *He understands*, Wolverine thought. It was nice to have a friend who understood him, even if he was silent.

Winter came, but the channel between Marble Island and the mainland did not freeze over completely. Mountains of ice moved with the tides and currents, crashing and flipping over as they collided with each other. The only living things that crossed that channel were the polar bears that scrambled over the moving ice and the seals that swam under it. And it got so cold, even Ukpigjuaq abandoned him for a time and migrated to warmer climates down south. He thought about Ukpigjuaq's wing. It reminded him of his uncle's arm—it gets cold sometimes but it is fine—he remembered his uncle telling him.

Every day, Wolverine climbed a hill and looked to the mainland. He had never been so lonely in his life. But eventually, spring returned and Ukpigjuaq with it. And, with the coming of spring, Wolverine thought about trying to go home again.

He decided he did not care if he could not set foot on the mainland. He would go there anyway. He would defy the magic. He would paddle his kayak until he reached the mainland, or he would perish somewhere between his lonely island and the mainland—and Breath. This thought stayed in his mind for a long time and worked its way into a conviction. It was a decision born of desperation.

One fine day, after the ice had left the west-end harbour, Wolverine said to his faithful companion, "I have been thinking, Mr. Ukpigjuaq. Let me tell you a story."

He told Ukpigjuaq the first story of Kiviuq. He told it as well as he remembered it. And then he said, "Well, Kiviuq paddled his kayak across the big ocean in a huge storm. When his kayak flipped over, he turned it back up again. He kept going until the wind finally stopped. If Kiviuq could do that, I can do it, too. Don't you think so?"

Of course, Ukpigjuaq did not answer. He just turned his head on its swivel and looked across the great divide to the mainland. He turned back and blinked his eyes twice, as if to say, "You have this crazy idea in your head. I think you are going to try it."

"What do you mean it is not a good idea, you miserable creature?" Wolverine laughed for the first time in a long time.

Ukpigjuaq only blinked.

But Wolverine's mind was made up; he was going home.

He went to prepare his kayak. He put new lashings in the frame where the braided sinew had worn or rotted with the weather. He repaired every hole he could find with needle and whale sinew. When he was finished, he launched his kayak into the west-end harbour and tied the splash guard tightly around his waist. He paddled out to deeper water and flipped his kayak over until he was underwater, and the bottom of the kayak was all that showed above water. He grabbed his paddle by one end and brought the other end down as hard as he could. There was a big splash but his kayak remained stubbornly upside down. He tried again. Still, his kayak did not right itself. *Be calm*, he said to himself. He let his paddle go and set to untying the line around his splash guard. With a big mouthful of water and bursting lungs, he finally climbed out of his kayak and came to the surface, spluttering for breath. He swam the short distance to the beach and dragged himself onto the rocks. As he choked and chucked up the last of the salt water in his lungs, Ukpigjuaq landed beside him and pecked at his head. "You silly boy," he seemed to be saying.

"I know," Wolverine said. "I forgot that part of the story. I have to learn to hold my breath."

Without getting up, Wolverine crawled back to the water. He took a deep breath and stuck his head in the water. When he could not hold his breath any longer, he lifted his head and took a deep breath. He looked at Ukpigjuaq with his very wet head and smiled. Ukpigjuaq lowered his head; he seemed to be saying "Do it again."

Wolverine said, "Yes sir!" He took a deep breath and stuck his head back in the water. Every time he lifted his head, Ukpigjuaq would bow his head, as if saying "Do it again." After dunking his head many times, Wolverine felt he could keep his head underwater long enough. He waded out and grabbed his kayak and his paddle and dragged them back. He turned his kayak over and emptied it out.

It took a few tries, and he nearly drowned a number of times, but eventually, he righted his kayak with his paddle. He did it again and again.

He spent the rest of the day flipping his kayak over and over again. By the end of the day, he was so tired, he fell asleep as soon as he entered his cave. The next day, he did it again, over and over and over again. He took another rest and then practised rolling his kayak day and night. By midsummer, he thought he could roll his kayak in his sleep. He rested and was ready.

The Way Home

On a calm day, Wolverine decided it was time to leave. He took his harpoon head and returned to his cave. He looked around. It was a place in which he had spent a whole winter: home. It saddened him to leave it. He had already packed all his belongings and taken them to the beach. The cave was bare except for the dry lichen and moss bed which he would leave for the next occupant. Satisfied, he said his last farewell, carefully put the harpoon head on a rock shelf, an offering of thanks to the cave (just as his father had said he must do), said, "Thank you," and left. He climbed up the wall of the big hole in the ground with the pool at the bottom of it. At the top, he took one last look around. It was clean and tidy. He walked along the rocky outcropping toward the little bay and his kayak.

He climbed into his kayak and tied his splash guard tightly around his waist. He made sure his hood was tight around his face. "We are going home!" he yelled to Ukpigjuaq, and dipped his paddle into the water.

He paddled around the south point of the island. A flock of guillemots flew by, barely above the water. He looked toward the rocky island. The rock face went straight up from the water. It was tinged with brown lichen clinging to the rock, making the white rock look, from a distance, like storm clouds gathering before the winds and rain came. As he turned toward the mainland, the wind picked up. He paddled on.

As he paddled, the wind got stronger and stronger. The waves got higher and higher. Soon there was a heavy gale blowing and the sea was white with foam. Still, Wolverine paddled on. Before long, he could see ahead of him nothing but a giant wall of water. He looked behind him and there was another wall of water. He climbed the wall in front of him and when he reached the top, it was like being on a mountaintop; he could see all around. There was the island and there was the mainland. He focussed on the mainland and dipped his paddle in the water with new determination. He descended into another valley of water and climbed up again. Soon, the waves began to break as they crested the hills, and came crashing down on Wolverine. He paid them no mind and paddled on.

A big wave came and flipped his kayak over. He took his paddle by the end and shoved the other end down into the depths of the sea with his other hand. His kayak rolled neatly back up. The journey had begun.

Wolverine battled the storm for a long time. Sometimes he was not sure whether he was right-side up or upside down, but he knew he was still alive and that made him happy. Sometimes he just had enough time to look ahead and take his bearings before another wave came crashing down on him. Sometimes he saw a hill on the mainland and thought he saw Breath standing on it. He paddled on.

He knew he was heading home and that made him happy. He knew he would see his mother and Little-loved-one and that made him happier still. And he knew he would see Breath and that made him happiest of all. He battled on. He knew not how long he paddled his kayak but it was a long time. Sometimes he wondered if he was awake or asleep. And sometimes, when he saw the mainland, he wondered if he was getting closer or not. But then, he decided it did not matter. He was not going back to the island. There was nothing to do but to battle on.

◆◆◆

Up at Fish River, The-man-with-no-eyebrows and his family knew something was afoot. One minute it was calm and the next, the wind had picked up, and now there was a gale blowing offshore. The sea was white with breaking waves.

"He is coming home," The-man-with-no-eyebrows said.

His wife could only say, "Yes."

When the wind blew into its second day, The-man-with-no-eyebrows, his wife, and even Little-loved-one knew Wolverine was determined to ride out the storm. The-man-with-no-eyebrows also knew that, as long as the wind blew, his son was paddling his kayak. He was alive out there in that storm. There was nothing he could do until the wind stopped. He could not paddle his kayak out into this storm to look for him. There was nothing to do but wait. His only fear was what he would find when the wind stopped.

Up above the waves Ukpigjuaq was also watching. He watched his friend paddling his kayak down below. He watched the kayak being thrown about in the big storm. He saw the bottom of the kayak and he saw his friend flip the kayak back up, as he had seen him do many times when Wolverine was practising his rolls. He saw him do it again and again. He did not know how many times he saw the bottom of the kayak, but he felt good when he saw his friend in the kayak. As long as he kept seeing his friend when the kayak rolled back up, he was happy.

Wolverine was tired and cold. The cold water seeped into his hood and down his back. But he kept going. His lips turned blue with cold, his hands were numb; he lost all feeling in his legs. Still, he paddled on. His only thought was of Breath and how he longed to see her again. Sometimes he dreamed about her: he saw her walking toward him, her smile so radiant in the sun, the way she bounced as she walked when she was happy, her long hair flowing in the breeze. He longed to see her so much, sometimes he thought he could almost touch her, and still, she seemed so far away.

On the third day, when Wolverine's kayak flipped over and he opened his eyes underwater, he could see seaweed. It stood up from the floor of the ocean, upside down, waving in the current. He could see a whole ocean of it all waving together, dancing for him. It was all so dreamy, just moving along there among the long, wavy seaweed. He decided it was not so bad; he could live there in the mysterious depths of the ocean. He looked down and saw a sculpin swimming along the bottom of the ocean. The sculpin swam so effortlessly, slowly moving its tail back and forth. He could swim along and chase that sculpin along the ocean floor. It would be fun. This was it. This was where he was destined to end his life, at the bottom of the bay where the mean boys were. He could play with them. They needed friends to play with, too. He saw a crab walking along the ocean floor. It was walking sideways as crabs always do. When his body lay along the ocean floor, that crab would come along and smell him all around. It would wait until he was completely dead and then it would open its claws . . .

A long piece of seaweed came at him and slapped him in the face. It stuck to his face and swiped it. It was long and flowed over his face, so smooth and slippery. He thought of what he was leaving behind. He thought of his father. His father had always been so nice to him. He had very patiently taught him how to cut a piece of walrus tusk ivory and shape it into a harpoon head. Now he would need another one because he had left his in the cave on the island. He thought of his mother, forever loving and caring. He thought of his little sister. He longed to take her into his arms and squeeze her in a big hug. And he thought of Breath walking away from the beach, away from his dead body, to cry alone, for him. Somehow the tip of the seaweed bit into his cheek and stung him. It hurt.

"Aakka—NO!!!" he yelled into the water.

He shoved his paddle into the water and forced it down with all his might. He did not have much strength left, but it was enough to right his kayak. He took a deep breath just as another wave hit him and turned his kayak back upside down. But he would not give in to the water again. He was glad he could feel, and he was glad it was cold and it stung his face. He would fight on. He was determined now.

A bird has to eat. Ukpigjuaq was getting hungry and there seemed to be no end in sight to the storm. Hunger gnawed at his stomach. He realized he had not eaten in three days, since his crazy friend had decided to paddle out in this storm. He had to eat something. He decided his friend would have to battle on his own for awhile. He had to eat. He flew back to Marble Island. He flew up high looking for lemmings with his keen eyes, but it was a lean year for lemmings and there are no siksiks on Marble Island. There was nothing to be found. He headed for the mainland.

Flying over the mainland, he searched for lemmings, but here, too, there were none to be found. He searched on. Finally, down among the rocks, he saw a siksik. He swooped down, and before the siksik even saw his shadow, he had grabbed it firmly in his talons. He flew to a hilltop to eat his catch. It was a scraggy old thing and it fought like a bear. It had hardly any meat on its bones and it was tough. And he noticed an old scar on its cheek. But a bird has to eat and lemmings and siksiks are an owl's favourite foods. He tore up the meagre flesh with his sharp beak and ate. And as he ate, he noticed that the weather had changed. The wind had stopped. The sea calmed. But he did not dwell on this thought; a bird had to eat, and a siksik is an owl's favourite food.

Way down on the sea, just to the north of Marble Island, Wolverine did not know if he had drowned or if he was just dreaming. The wind seemed to have stopped. The sea was calm. Rolling, shiny gentle swells rose and fell around him, the aftermath of a heavy storm. He seemed to be waking up. There was his father in front of him, paddling his own kayak, tied to Wolverine's, pulling him toward the mainland. It was a wonderful sight.

He looked up at the sky and smiled. Where was Ukpigjuaq? The sky was so beautiful. Somehow, the curse was broken and he was going home. *Breath, Breath, Breath* . . . he kept saying to himself. He was going to see Breath. He put his head back on his chest, and before he could think another pleasant thought, he was fast asleep again.

Setting Foot on the Land Again

The next time Wolverine woke, he and his father were almost ashore at Fish River. Little-loved-one waded out with a ladleful of fresh water for them to drink. Wolverine drank heartily. When he came ashore, his legs were wobbly; he staggered when he walked. He went into his parents' tent, removed his wet clothes, and lay down on the bed. He lay there and slept for what seemed like a week. And he dreamed. He dreamed of paddling his kayak, rising and falling in the gentle swells. Sometimes he opened his eyes, but his eyelids were so heavy he had to close them again. His body ached. He felt he needed to do something but he could not lift his arms; he could not get up. His body felt so heavy. Sometimes he woke and heard his mother singing:

My boy
My little growing boy
What did you see today?
Aiyaa yai yaa

Did you see the baby geese
The baby geese
Did they make you all wet
Ayaa yaa

Soon they will grow and fly away
Far, far away
They do that
Ayaa yaa

Soon you will leave me
And travel with your father
You will do that
Ayaa yaa ... .

It was a song he remembered from a dream, a long time ago. He felt like a little boy again. And he dreamed of Breath. When he finally opened his eyes, Little-loved-one was looking at him, her chin cupped in her hands, a big smile on her face.

Wolverine smiled and said, "What are you doing?"

"Waiting," she said.

"Waiting for what?" Wolverine asked.

"Waiting for you to say 'Breath' again," Little-loved-one said, and laughed. "Breath, Breath, Breath . . ." she teased.

"Oh, you," Wolverine said and grabbed her. He tickled her and they laughed. He held his little sister by her shoulders at arm's length and looked at her. "Look at you," he said. "How big you are. Soon, someone will come and take *you* away for a wife."

Little-loved-one blushed. "No!" she said, firmly. "I am always going to stay with my anaanak—my mother."

Wolverine said, "No, you're not. There is that boy who lives way up inland at that big lake. Someday soon, he will come and take you away."

"I am never going up there, never. I am never going to marry anyone," Little-loved-one said. And she attacked her brother again.

"Breath, Breath . . ." she teased.

When they had finally settled down, Wolverine asked his father, "What happened? I thought I could not set foot on this land."

His father said, "You were out in the storm for three days. When the wind finally stopped, I went out and found you. I tied a line to your kayak and pulled you back. You were no help at all. You slept all the way home. You kept mumbling something about breathing. And you were smiling. You were smiling even in your sleep."

His father laughed a knowing laugh. Wolverine blushed and everyone had a good laugh.

He looked around him. His mother seemed older somehow. There were worry lines on her face that became pronounced when she smiled. His father looked wise and tall. Little-loved-one was a whole year older, such a big girl. He squeezed her in a very long hug.

"But what about the curse?" he asked his father. "What happened to the curse? I am here, on the mainland."

The-man-with-no-eyebrows answered, "I hear Paaliaq has lost his powers completely. His tuurngaq seems to have gone, probably killed by some hungry animal. But he is not unhappy about that. His tuurngaq was not paying him any attention at all. He will get himself another, a more agreeable one."

Wolverine asked, "Where are they now?"

"They are up at In-there, fishing. I think we should go up there. You have to get up and do something before you get too lazy; you have been sleeping for days," his father said.

And that is what they did. They packed their things and trekked up to In-there. Wolverine saw Breath and blushed, thinking about the thoughts he had had about her when he was away. She was so beautiful. She blushed, too, thinking her own private thoughts. They did not see each other much the rest of that summer. He was busy, out hunting with his father. She spent most of her time working with her mother.

In the fall, Paaliaq's family went south again and The-man-with-no-eyebrows and his family went north.

And They Lived . . .

It was a very good winter. There was plenty of game to be had. The caribou were fat and the seals had good skins. As the days got longer toward spring, people began to gather at Bit-of-sand, not by any real choice to gather, but because they just happened by there and liked the company. Breath and her family were there. The-man-with-no-eyebrows' family arrived there one day and built their igloo. They fed their dogs and settled down. When they woke up each morning and went outside, a new igloo or two had sprung up during the night, until there were a dozen or so igloos, haphazardly placed on the gently sloping ground. The people slept late and visited each other late into the night. There was no need to hunt. They had plenty of food. There was much merrymaking.

One day, Paaliaq came out of his igloo carrying a snow-knife and looked at the sky. It was blue and the sun was high. It would be a good day to spend outside.

"Qaggi!," he yelled at the top of his lungs to the camp in general. "Party!"

Other people came out of their igloos, carrying snow-knives. Soon, the whole community had come out to help: men, women, some carrying babies on their backs, and children. They had come to build a giant party igloo called a qaggi. They gathered on a level spot.

"Here!" Paaliaq said. "We will build the qaggi here."

He walked in a wide circle, drawing a line with his snow-knife as he walked. There was a festive atmosphere about the place. People began cutting blocks of snow out of the ground. Soon they had an assembly line going. Half a dozen men were cutting blocks of snow. Another half-dozen were putting up the blocks, building the walls of the giant igloo. And between the block cutters and the wall builders, a long line of people passed the blocks, hand to hand, toward the igloo. There was much chatter and joking among the caribou-skin-clad crowd. Someone cut a hole, down on the side of the igloo, which became the doorway. Through this hole, the blocks now disappeared only to reappear up on the side of the igloo. As the walls rose, others piled snow inside the igloo for the wall builders to stand on.

The walls rose higher and higher, as block after block went up in a spiral.

When the main igloo was completed, the men began to build smaller ones all around the giant igloo, connecting them to the main igloo by short tunnels. Women and children shovelled snow up the sides of the igloo, filling in the cracks between the blocks. Here, too, there was an assembly line of sorts: someone on the ground would pick up a shovelful of snow throw it up to a person standing precariously on the side of the igloo, who would catch the flying snow with her shovel and throw it up to the next person, until the shovelful of snow finally landed on the side of the igloo, where it was tamped down with another shovel. And so the work continued throughout the day until the igloos were all completed and cleaned out of excess snow.

Wolverine and Breath came to help, too. They could not keep their eyes away from each other. They would look at each other and smile. They did not go near one another. They only looked at each other and smiled a lot.

When the igloos were finished, the people continued preparing for their festival. They stood the two longest sleds they had into the ground and stretched a strong rope across them. They anchored the ends of the rope to the ground. The rope was so tight one could walk across it if one was a tightrope walker. It was evening when the preparations were finally completed.

With the sun slowly sinking in the west, everyone gathered in the party igloo. People told stories about what had happened with them throughout the winter. Paaliaq's mother told another Kiviuq story to the children gathered around her. His wife showed the children how to play with string.

Someone said, "Everybody! Quiet please!"

Everyone looked in the direction of the speaker. It was Paaliaq who had spoken. Everyone quietened down.

"Only a few short winters ago," Paaliaq said, "The-man-with-no-eyebrows came to me and asked for my daughter. I am sorry to say I was not in a very good mood that day and refused his offer of a good husband for my daughter."

The people laughed; they all knew Paaliaq's reputation.

"But, being the good-natured soul that I am," Paaliaq continued as people laughed some more, "I asked him, sometime later, if I could have his son for my son-in-law. The good man said 'Yes' to my humble request, and I am now proud to have such a fine young man for a son-in-law-to-be."

Wolverine blushed a very deep red.

Paaliaq continued "Today, I would like to honour my word and give my daughter to this young man, if he will have her. Wolverine, my daughter, Breath, I give to you.

May you live and be happy together for many winters to come. And give me many grandchildren."

Wolverine looked at Breath, a lump in his throat. His legs would not work. They wobbled when he tried to stand up. He remained sitting. Breath looked at him, her face red. She could not move either.

"Along with Breath," Paaliaq continued, filling in the embarrassed silence between his daughter and his son-in-law, "I would like to give you my sled to send you on your way to a good life."

"He will have to wait 'til after this party to take your sled," someone said. "It is holding up the tightrope."

They all laughed.

The-man-with-no-eyebrows stood up with tears in his eyes. "Thank you, Paaliaq," he said. "And, My Son, you can pick your dogs from my team to pull your sled."

The-man-with-no-eyebrows could not talk anymore. He was stricken with such happiness it made him speechless. He sat down.

Wolverine finally found his legs and walked over to Breath. He took her hand. She stood up. He brushed his nose to her left ear and sniffed. Oh, how wonderful she smelled. Very quietly, he said, "Wife," and squeezed her hand.

"Husband," she replied.

To all the cheers and hoots and hollers from every-one, Wolverine and Breath retired to one of the small connecting igloos to be alone for a while. They were now husband and wife.

There was a great feast that evening. Everyone brought food, which was passed around from person to person. People would cut a piece of food off and pass the rest on to the next person. And steaming pots of soup passed among the crowd until people were all so stuffed they had to crawl into the adjoining igloos to snooze awhile. When they were rested, they came back for more.

Someone had brought a drum. One of the men put a skin on the drum. A group of people sat in a circle, feet together in the middle, holding the frame of the drum. Slowly, they turned the drum around and around, tightening the string holding the skin in place. This done, Paaliaq tuned the drum with a stick and placed it on the floor in the middle of the room. A chant started:

> *"Aijaa, ajaijaa, ijja, jijja quvianaqquuq . . .*
> *What is happiness, ajaijaa . . .*
>
> *When the moon shines and the dogs trot,*
> *The sled creaks over the snow*
> *My mind begins to wander and what*
> *It is I do not know*
> *Ajai jaa . . .*

Aijaa . . .
Makes my chest swell with wonder
A song comes to me
What was it over yonder
That my eyes should see
Ajai jaa . . .

Aijaa . . .
But that beautiful inlet beyond
Where the caribou roam
And wolverines and their young
Make their home
Ajai jaa . . .

Paaliaq went up to the drum, picked it up, and began to beat it with the knocker, slowly, up and down on the frame. When he hit it on the bottom, it twisted down; when he hit it on the top, it twisted up. The sound echoed on the walls of the giant igloo, *boom, boom,* and the people sang, "*Ajai jaa . . . ajai jaa . . .*" The dance went late into the night.

The next day, there were games of strength: arm twisting and wrestling. There were games on the tightrope outside. Men climbed up on the rope to their midsection. With the rope held firmly in each hand, they rolled over the rope, forward, keeping the rope in their mid-section, until they were back in the same position they started in, twisting around and around. It was a test to see who could twist around the most number of times without tiring, a test of endurance.

There was much joking. "A little tired, are you?" they taunted Wolverine. "Did you not get much sleep?"

Breath did not fare much better with the women. She sat through most of the day, daydreaming.

"A bit sleepy, are we? What are you dreaming about?" they teased her, slapping her on her back.

The only thing to do was to blush and smile and ignore all the jokes.

There was much merrymaking all around. In the evening, there was a soccer game on the sea ice. The game went on all night, the people running all over the sea ice that was their soccer field. Sometimes they were miles away from the goals. When they got hungry, they feasted. And so the party went. It went on for many days and nights.

When it was finally over, Wolverine and Breath took their sled down. Wolverine chose his dogs. His mother gave them clothing that she had made for them and gave Breath a needle and needle case. Auk gave them a qulliq. With these few things, they would start their lives together. They said their good-byes.

Breath sat on the sled. Wolverine drove their few dogs along the shore. Down by the sea on their right, they could see the white island, Marble Island. Wolverine thought about his year on the island and his longing for the day when he and Breath would finally be together. And now, here they were, travelling away to start a new life. Wolverine smiled. "Hut, hut!" he said to the dogs, urging them on. They turned left and headed north.

Taima

Afterword

I would like to declare, here and now, that the comments I make in this book about shamanism are based entirely on my own views and suppositions. I do not profess to have any knowledge upon the matter whatsoever. As kids, we played at being shamans, of course, waving our arms about, calling, "Pamiuq, pamiuq. . . ." But it was all child's fancy.

Having said that, I would like to say that the world of shamans was a real world, practised by ordinary people. Some were good people, some a bit misguided. The last shaman of whom I had personal knowledge died three or four years ago. He was one of the nicest people I ever knew. I hope I have not done a disservice to him and his kind.

M.A.K

Acknowledgements

I would like to thank, first and foremost, a friend mine, Joachim Kavik, a wonderful artist who works in stone. Kavik lives here in Rankin Inlet. When I was looking for names for my characters, I happened upon him at the Co-op. I asked him if I could use his name, Kavik, and his father's name, Kabluitok, in my book. I explained to him that I would translate them into English, the way Indians translate theirs: Sitting Bull, Melting Tallow, and such. He laughed in that good-natured way of his and said, "Of course. We artists have to help each other out whenever we can." My main characters, Wolverine and The-man-with-no-eyebrows, although they are completely and absolutely creations of my own imagination and bear neither resemblance nor relation to Kavik or Kabluitok, are named after them. I hope I have done justice to their names.

This book began to take shape in Dawson City, Yukon, where I was writer-in-residence at the famous writer and philanthropist Pierre Berton's childhood home. I am sad to say Mr. Berton is no longer among us, but he had the generosity and forethought to donate his house so that wayward writers like me could develop their stories in incredible surroundings. (Robert Service's cabin is directly across the street.) My thanks, also, to the Klondike Visitors Association, whose members made all the arrangements and made my residency one of the most pleasurable experiences in my writing career. I would also like to thank all those wonderful librarians at the Dawson City Public Library. I bothered them daily for information, some of which must have seemed completely irrelevant to anything anyone would need, but they produced them nonetheless. Librarians are my favourite people.

My education is lacking when it comes to girls; I do not have any. So I enlisted the help of my good friend Janet Tamalik (Has-it-all) McGrath to enlighten me on how girls grow up in Inuit society. She grew up among Inuit, way up north. Tamalik is a young Qablunaaq woman on the outside, but inside, she is a wise Inuk.

I would also like to thank Lynne Missen, the only editor I have had the pleasure to work with.

Finally, I would like to give a special thank-you to a beautiful young friend of mine, Keira Keil, my Kukuk (Chocolate), a librarian's daughter. She came to visit me in Dawson City at spring break when she was seven. Every day, she brought me cups of steaming coffee as I worked. I am sure the floorboards of Berton House are still stained with the coffee she spilled.

M.A.K.